NOVELS BY MAX ALLAN COLLINS:

Midnight Haul
The Million-Dollar Wound
A Shroud for Aquarius
True Crime
Kill Your Darlings
True Detective
No Cure for Death
The Baby Blue Rip-Off
Scratch Fever
Hard Cash
Hush Money
Fly Paper
Quarry's Cut
(formerly: The Slasher)
Quarry's Deal
(formerly: The Dealer)
Quarry's List
(formerly: The Broker's Wife)
Quarry
(formerly: The Broker)
Blood Money
Bait Money

midnight haul

Max Allan Collins

A Foul Play Press Book
THE COUNTRYMAN PRESS
Woodstock
Vermont

Library of Congress Cataloging-in-Publication Data

Collins, Max Allan.
Midnight haul.

"Foul Play Press book."
I. Title
PS3553.04753M5   1986   813'.54   86-16626
ISBN 0-88150-077-1

Text design by Wladislaw Finne

for
Barb
and
Nate

"I know it don't thrill you,
I hope it don't kill you:
welcome to the working week."

— ELVIS COSTELLO

one
forewarning

1

Neighbors on either side heard the shots. They called the police, but Ray Turner, who was one-fourth of Greenwood, New Jersey's P.D., had heard the shots too and was running across the grade-school playground, barren in the moonlight, his gun drawn.

It was just after midnight. Turner, tall, thin, twenty-six, was walking around the school, checking doors, poking in windows with his longbeam flash. He was moving a little slow tonight; the day had been hot and humid and the night was no better: moving through air like this was like walking underwater.

So he was a little behind schedule tonight, not that it mattered. Things in Greenwood didn't move fast. No pressure, here. That's what he liked about it. That's why he'd come home to Greenwood, after an unpleasant few years as a Newark cop.

Only now he was running across the playground, the thick air grabbing at his lungs, goddamn cigarettes, gun in one hand, flash in the other, and what the fuck was that? *Another* shot?

He slowed as he reached the wire mesh fence separating the playground from the row of tract homes; the one directly in front of him, the one he was heading for, belonged to Jack Brock, a man

1

Turner knew, to speak to. A truck driver out at the Kemco plant.

The fence was only waist high, but it seemed to take forever to scale. He was sweating. Drenched in it. Ahead of him the Brock house was dark. Not a light on in the place. Of course the neighbors' lights were on, but nobody was standing around outside: gunshots make people curious, not crazy. Their lights, and the moonlight, helped him dodge the toys littered around the Brocks' backyard: a wagon, a trike, a wading pool.

Two shots, there'd been. Spaced perhaps thirty seconds apart. Then, maybe a minute later, a minute Turner had spent making his way here, there'd been another. Three shots.

The foundation was built up from the ground, with a back door entering onto a lower, basement floor. He flattened himself to the cement wall, the door to his left. He was shaking. Breathing hard.

His back to the foundation, he reached over, flash tucked in his armpit, and tried the screen door. Unlocked. He opened it a hair, slid his foot in to keep it open. Then, using his foot, he eased it all the way open until he was facing the inside door, which he tried.

Locked.

"Shit," he said, very softly, and kicked it in.

He went in low, fanning the gun around like goddamn Clint Eastwood, and the flashlight, too, revealing nothing but a damp basement with washer and drier and, in one dry area, some more scattered toys. The air smelled sickly sweet, from a room deodorizer, probably. An open wooden stairway was right across from him, waiting for him. Daring him to come up.

He stood and listened for a minute, then, hearing nothing, took the dare.

2

He made very little noise, going up; the hum of the air-conditioning upstairs covered him. But he felt uneasy following the beam of light up the steps. He was starting to wish he'd stayed in Newark.

There was a landing, and a jog to the left, then five more steps and a door. He opened it, quickly, and only the bottom half opened — a damn Dutch door — the upper half catching him and he fell backwards, tumbling down the steps.

The landing saved him. He wasn't hurt, but he was disoriented; after a few seconds, he pushed up and went back up the five steps, in a crouch, looking up through the open bottom half of the door, probing with the flash. He ducked under the closed upper door and was in the kitchen, modest, modern, empty.

It was cold in here, air-conditioner doing overtime, but that didn't make it any easier to breathe: fear had hold of Turner's chest, and as he moved into the living room, the beam of the flash betrayed his shaking hand. He tried to guide the light steadily, quickly around the room, but the effect was more like a strobe. The strobe effect picked up early American furniture, a family portrait over a spinet, a shape on the floor by the front door.

Turner pointed the gun and the light at the shape and saw blood.

He choked back vomit. Moved closer, but did so keeping his back to the shape, in case whoever had done this was still in the house: the flash lit up a hallway, off to the left, an empty hallway, and he saw no one.

No one except the dead woman on the floor, on her side. A woman about thirty, in curlers and a pink robe. Her face was all there, and rather pretty, turned as if to look at him, one empty eye looking across blood at him; it was a face he'd glimpsed in that family portrait. Most of the back of her head was gone. Some of it was on the door.

He turned back toward that hallway, wishing to Christ he'd stayed in Newark. Wishing it wasn't so cold, so fucking cold in here. He walked down the hallway. Slow.

On the right, an open door: bathroom. Stool, sink, tub with shower curtain open; nobody in there.

Another open door: sewing room. Small. Empty.

And another: a kid's room; Star Wars wallpaper. He pointed gun and flash in there.

And quickly pulled the flash away, hoping he would be able someday to forget what he'd seen: a boy, about ten, with a bloody face, head spilled open like a broken melon on the red-sodden pillow. Bloody matter on the wall behind him, on Luke Skywalker and Chewbacca, and Christ, it took a big gun to do that. Jesus.

Across the hall, in a room wallpapered with blue flowers, a girl, perhaps seven, dead.

He stood in the hall, gun and flash pointed down, and felt anger rise in him like heat, pushing the nausea out. He could feel himself breathing hard. His teeth were clenched so tight they hurt. But he couldn't unclench them. He didn't want to.

At the end of the hall, one last door.

Closed.

He kicked it open.

The gun and the flash pointed right at the man sitting on the edge of the double bed. About thirty-five, balding, a little heavy. He was wearing boxer shorts. There was a gun in his lap. A .357 magnum.

The man was Jack Brock. There was some blood spattered on him.

"Did you do this, Jack?" Turner heard himself say.

4

Brock didn't say anything; his face looked slack, flesh hanging like dough.

"Why, Jack?"

Brock put his hand on the gun in his lap.

"Don't, Jack!"

Brock left his hand on the gun. He looked up at Turner and said, "They killed my wife."

"What?"

"They killed my wife. My kids. I tried to save my kids."

"Take your hand off the gun, Jack."

"They'd kill me next, if I let them."

"Put it down, Jack. Down!"

Brock raised the gun.

"Jack. I don't want to shoot you, Jack. Jack!"

Brock looked down the barrel of the gun and squeezed the trigger and there was a red explosion.

2

It didn't make any sense to Crane. *He* was the serious one; *he* was the one who got occasionally depressed. Mary Beth had always kidded him out of his moods. "Hey asshole," she'd say. "Don't take life so serious." And now, suicide? Mary Beth? Didn't make sense.

His friend Roger Beatty had driven him from Iowa City to Cedar Rapids, where he could catch the plane that would take him to New Jersey; he'd have to take a bus from there to Greenwood, Mary Beth's hometown, the East Coast equivalent of his own small hometown in Iowa, Wilton Junction. Or at least that's how Mary Beth had described it to him: "That's why we have so much in common, Crane: we grew up in the same town — only where you come from they sound like Henry Fonda, and where I come from it's strictly Rodney Dangerfield."

He smiled at the sound of her voice as it drifted through his head; it didn't sound anything like Rodney Dangerfield. Then he felt his smile fade and wondered why he hadn't wept yet. He looked out the window of the plane and a large chemical plant far below was making its own clouds beneath the others.

"Suicide happens," Roger had told him in the car. Roger was Crane's age, twenty-two, a slightly overweight, dark-haired guy, with thick glasses and the

9

absent-mindedly sloppy appearance of somebody scientific, which he was, sort of: Roger was majoring in sociology. He'd apparently had some psych, too, because he had, in a well-meaning but irritating way, given Crane a mini-lecture on the subject of suicide.

"You don't have to be depressed your whole life to commit suicide," Roger said. "Just one day. Or night, or afternoon. But it only takes once."

"Roger," Crane said. "I don't want to talk about this right now."

"You got to, sooner or later."

"Make it later."

Now it was later, on the plane, and he still didn't want to talk — or think — about it. But there it was: Mary Beth, twenty, dead. Mary Beth, long brown hair, wide brown eyes, wry little smile, supple little body, gone.

He pressed the heels of his hands against his forehead and sat forward in his seat.

"You okay, man?"

Crane turned and looked at the passenger in the next seat. Actually, there was an empty seat between them, here in second class, and that was okay with Crane: he didn't care to make conversation, particularly not with another college student, this one a bearded longhaired throwback to the '60s, in jeans and gray T-shirt, some jerk who thought Kent State happened last week.

"Need an aspirin or something?" the guy was saying. "I can go get the flight attendant for you."

"No. That's okay." Why was he thinking this guy was a jerk? He was nice enough. The jerk.

"My name's Phil Stanley," the guy said, and held out his hand.

After just a moment, Crane took the hand, got

10

caught in a sideways "soul" shake, and said, "My name's Crane."

"You a student, too?"

"Yes."

"Headed back to school, huh? Where d'you go?"

"Actually, no. I go to Iowa. Graduate student — fall semester starts in a few weeks and I'm, uh . . ."

"Taking advantage of your last few weeks' vacation. For sure. Don't blame ya."

"Right."

"What you taking?"

"I'm a journalism major."

"No shit? Me too. Or anyway, sort of — I'm into broadcast journalism."

The guy would have to clean up his image if he wanted to go on camera, Crane thought, then, noticing the guy was expecting him to report back, said, "I'm in print media."

"Oh, yeah? What's your specialty?"

"I don't know yet. Maybe investigative."

"One thing this country'll never run out of," the guy said, shaking his mangy head, "is Watergates."

Crane hated it when people invoked Watergate after he told them he was interested in investigative reporting. Maybe he could remember to quit telling people that. Maybe he should say he was interested in writing sports or something.

"That's the ticket," the guy was saying. "Keep the fuckin' government on its toes."

"And big business," Crane said. "Don't forget big business."

"Right on," the guy said.

Right on? Did that guy *really* say "right on"? Why do people like this always assume you're liberal? And if you tell them you believe in the system, that you

11

don't see anything wrong with capitalism, why do they make you out as some sort of right-wing lunatic?

"Because," Mary Beth used to say, "you *are* one. You think you're middle-of-the road, mainstream America. A political moderate. Sure you are. Compared to the Ku Klux Klan. How many black folks you got in Wilton Junction? You never called anybody nigger 'cause you never saw one, except on TV. You're just a reactionary hick, Crane, and I'm gonna educate you if I have to spend the rest of my life doing it . . ."

"Are you *sure* you're okay?" the bearded guy was asking.

"Maybe I will take that aspirin," Crane said.

The guy rose to go find a flight attendant.

Crane sat back in his seat and thought about the fight he and Mary Beth had had their first night together. He was living in an apartment that was actually half a house, a duplex, sharing it with three other guys who were gone for the weekend. He'd only known Mary Beth for a few weeks; he was a senior and she was a sophomore, and both had been at the University for over a year, Crane having transferred from Port City Community College just as she was enrolling as a freshman. But it was a big campus with a lot of students, and until some mutual friends introduced them they'd never even seen each other. He liked her sense of humor, and (one of the mutual friends told him) she liked his sandy brown hair and freckles; thought he had a nice, innocent look.

Which was what the fight was about, really.

He'd planned to seduce her, and that was a major step for him, requiring a lot of strategy, and making him very nervous, because he was less experienced than he supposed most other twenty-year-old males in this country to be. So he had cooked an Italian dinner for her (her favorite, and his), bought a Phoebe

12

Snow album (her favorite — *hardly* his), dimmed the lights prior to her arrival, and found himself naked on the couch with her before the first course of the meal and without even taking the plastic wrapper off the goddamn Phoebe Snow album.

He was proud of himself, though — he didn't come right away, like he thought he would; after all, it was his first time, and most people, on their first time, come right away. Not him. Which was something, anyway.

Of course it clearly wasn't *her* first time, and that was part of what the fight was about, too.

"It was your first time, wasn't it?" she said later, nibbling her lasagna.

"You weren't supposed to know that," he said, smiling a little.

"Hey, you did fine. Most guys come right away, their first time. You didn't."

"Neither did you."

"Well I did in the long run, and that's something, anyway."

And they'd both smiled and finished their lasagna and wine and listened to Phoebe Snow (which he even sort of liked, at this point) and made love another time. Finally they watched a late movie about vampires — one of those sexy British ones from the '60s — and that's when the fight started.

"It sure wasn't *your* first time," he said. Out of nowhere. Surprised by the petulance in his own voice.

"I never said it was," she said, still smiling, but on the edge of not.

"No big deal."

"I'm glad you see it that way."

"I do. It's no big fucking deal."

"Hey, ain't *we* profane all of a sudden. 'Farm boy says fuck.' Stop the presses!"

"Don't you make fun of me."

"Then don't *you* insult *me*."

"All I said was—"

"Hey. Make you a deal."

"What?"

"Don't give me a bad time about not being a virgin, and I won't give you a bad time about being one."

"Well fuck you!"

She smiled again. "That's the general idea, yes."

And the fight was over.

When he woke the next morning she was playing with his hair.

"I like playing with your hair," she said.

"You like my freckles, too."

"I suppose Fran told you that."

Fran was one of the mutual friends.

"Yeah, she did."

She smiled, crinkling her chin. "I'd like to get my hands on the little bitch . . ."

"Me, too."

She hit him with a pillow. Not hard.

"Don't," she said. Kidding on the square.

"Don't what?"

"Don't be with anybody else. Not Fran or anybody."

"I wasn't serious . . ."

"I know. But I am. I won't be with anybody else from now on, and you just be with me. Understand?"

He'd understood. They'd been together since then. Lived together, starting last school year. They'd had the normal squabbles any couple has, but nothing serious; Mary Beth had been loving and sarcastically cheerful throughout. Though they'd never met, Mary Beth's mother (her father died a few years before)

14

seemed to approve of him and of the relationship—which had become an engagement; his parents loved Mary Beth and even seemed resigned to the wedding being held in New Jersey.

But the need for both Crane and Mary Beth to work had separated them this summer. He'd been working construction, and she'd gone home, to Greenwood, NJ, where she had a summer job lined up. They'd spoken on the phone at least once a week, usually more often . . .

"Here's that aspirin," the bearded guy was saying. He was handing a paper cup of water and two packaged tablets to Crane, who said, "Thank you very much," and meant it.

"Listen," the guy said. "If I'm out of line, say so: but I can tell something's bothering you, and it's an hour and a half yet to New Jersey, so if you want to talk, it's fine with me. And if not, that's fine too . . ."

"Thanks, no," Crane said. Then felt compelled—perhaps out of guilt for calling somebody this considerate a jerk, even to himself—to add, "I'm not on a vacation. Someone close to me died recently. I'm going East for the funeral."

"Hey, man. I'm very sorry. Really."

"It's okay. I just need to sit here quietly—if you don't mind."

"You got it. Why not put on the 'phones and just relax?" The guy was referring to the headsets they'd been given that could be plugged into the armrest for a dozen channels of music and such.

"Maybe I will," Crane said, taking the headset out of its plastic wrapper.

"There ya go," the guy said, smiling, nodding.

It had been a week since he'd talked to her last, when she killed herself; razor blades . . . Jesus, razor blades.

15

She was still wearing his engagement ring; she'd be buried with it, tomorrow. No note. Nothing. No reason.

But there had to be. A reason. He had to know what it was. He wouldn't leave that goddamn town till he knew what it was.

He put the headphones on and heard "You Light Up My Life," as arranged for elevators. He switched channels, thinking, just my luck, I'll get Phoebe Snow. He hit the comedy station and heard Rodney Dangerfield.

He began to weep.

3

At the funeral, he didn't weep.

Crane just sat there, feeling out of place. The people in the pews around him were strangers, and almost all of them old. He'd never met Mary Beth's mother before, and she was as much a stranger as any of them; the fact that Mary Beth's eyes were in the face of this plump, fiftyish woman seemed somehow nothing more than an odd coincidence. He was alone in a church full of people, none of whom he knew, except for Mary Beth. And she was dead.

Yesterday, he'd walked two miles into town from the truck stop where the bus from the airport had deposited him. He'd come to New Jersey expecting a landscape cluttered with fast-food restaurants, gas stations, billboards, one big sprawling city with no houses, just industries belching smoke, highways intersecting at crazy angles, traffic endless in all directions.

What he found was green, rolling farmland that could've been Iowa.

He'd come down over a hill, walking along a blacktop road, and there, in the midst of a Grant Wood landscape, was Greenwood. Or so the water tower said. He saw one gas station (Fred's Mobil) and one fast-food restaurant (Frigid Queen) and a John Deere dealership, before reaching a single, modest billboard that welcomed him to "New Jersey's Cleanest Little City," courtesy of the Chamber of Commerce, three churches and two fraternal lodges. Just past the billboard was a power and water facility and a sign that gave the population: 6000.

Still on the outskirts, he passed twenty or so modern homes, off to the left; the land was very flat here, the only trees looking small and recently planted and underfed. The lack of foliage was emphasized by the homes being spread further apart than they'd be in a similar development in a larger city. Crane's parents lived in a house like that, on the outskirts of Wilton Junction.

None of this made him feel at home; rather, he felt an uneasiness, and had retreated to a motel, barely within the Greenwood city limits, without even phoning Mary Beth's mother to let her know he was in town. There he watched television till his eyes burned, none of it registering, but helping keep his mind empty of what had brought him here.

He even managed to sleep. Eventually.

The next morning, *this* morning, he woke at eleven and called Mary Beth's house. He knew the funeral was at one, but he didn't know how to get there. An aunt answered the phone and gave him directions. He showered, shaved, got dressed for the occasion, and sat in a chair and stared at a motel wall for nearly two hours. The wall was yellow — painted, not papered — and there was a window with an air conditioner and green drapes in the middle of the wall. There was also a crooked picture, a print, of a small girl sitting beside a lake under a tree in summer. It was a pleasant enough picture, but it bothered him it was crooked. He straightened it before he left to walk into town to the church for the funeral.

The casket was open, and he'd overheard several people saying how pretty Mary Beth looked, and, inevitably, that she looked like she was sleeping. But Crane had seen dead people before and none of them had looked asleep to him. The father of a close friend of his in high school had died in a terrible fiery car crash, and his casket had been open at the funeral, displayed up by the door as you exited, so you couldn't avoid looking at the admirable but futile attempt the mortician had made at making his friend's father look like his friend's father.

He and his friend and his friend's father had spent two weeks three summers in a row at a lodge in the Ozarks; the lodge was more an elaborate hotel posing as a lodge than a lodge, and his friend's father, who had money from a construction business, the same construction business Crane worked for this and other summers, was generous and fun to be with. Crane had spent many hours with the man. But now, whenever he thought of his friend's father, he saw the face of the car crash victim in the open casket.

So he did not go up to the front of the church to see Mary Beth one last time. In the future, when he thought of Mary Beth, he wanted to think of Mary Beth.

The wood in the long narrow Presbyterian church was dark; the stained-glass windows, with their stilted scenes, let in little light. Even the minister, a thin, middle-aged man, was making his innocuous comments about this young woman, with whom he'd barely been acquainted, in a deep, resonant voice, its tones as dark as the woodwork.

Right now he was saying something — "a gentle person, thoughtful, kind" — that might have pertained to anyone, outside of Adolph Hitler or Mike Wallace. And Crane's mind began wandering, and he glanced

19

down toward the left, three rows up from him, at the back of the head of the blonde girl. Or woman. Crane had a hunch she was the type who'd consider "girl" a sexist word. That was okay. He didn't consider "sexist" a word.

She seemed so out of place here. Even more so than him. At least he was wearing a suit, wrinkled as it was from being stuffed in his one small suitcase. But among all these people in their forties, fifties, sixties, seventies, wearing their Sunday best, this blonde girl, woman, whatever, with jeans and an old plaid shirt . . .

He'd watched when she came in, a little late, and he was watching her now, the back of her head, side of her face. Good-looking girl. Woman. Cute face, no makeup. Nice body, no bra.

Jesus: he was getting a hard-on.

He crossed his legs. Tried to cross his legs. Folded his hands in his lap, feeling uncomfortable and ashamed. But he could hear an amused Mary Beth saying, "A hard-on at my funeral? Very classy behavior, asshole." At least that's how *his* Mary Beth would've reacted; he didn't know how the Mary Beth who killed herself would react. He didn't know that Mary Beth at all.

The moment passed, and so did the casket, brought up the aisle by the pallbearers, men in their forties and fifties, nameless relatives all, and now the only thing Crane felt was empty.

It was good to get outside, in the sunshine. Cool, crisp, early fall day. Football weather soon. Iowa City. It would be nice to get back to Iowa City . . . if Mary Beth were there . . .

They were putting Mary Beth into the hearse. That is, the pallbearers were, with the guiding hand of someone from the funeral home, putting the casket in the back of the black Cadillac.

This isn't happening, he thought.

"I suppose you don't have a car."

He turned. The blonde girl—woman—in the plaid shirt and jeans was standing there. He felt a rush of embarrassment.

"Do you always blush at funerals?" she asked. Her voice wasn't particularly friendly. It was, in fact, coldly sarcastic.

"I . . . don't know you . . ." Crane stammered.

"You're Crane. You'd have to be. I'm Boone."

"Boone?"

"It's my last name. My first name is Anne, but let's just keep it Crane and Boone, okay? I got a car."

"Huh?"

"A car. I got a car. You want to be in the funeral procession or what?"

"I'd like to be at the graveside, yes, when they . . ."

"Then come on."

She had a little yellow Datsun, a couple years old, and she opened the door on the rider's side for him and he got in.

"You were a friend of Mary Beth's?" he asked her.

"I still am."

"Nobody else her age was there."

"I wasn't her age. I'm older than she was. And I'm older than you, too."

"Oh."

They found a place in the line of cars. Boone switched her lights on. A five-minute drive brought them to Greenwood Cemetery in the country, amidst more Grant Wood scenery.

Crane stood near the grave as a few more words were spoken and the casket was lowered into the ground. Boone stayed back by her car.

Mary Beth's mother approached Crane and said, "Please stop by the house before you leave town," and turned away, a male relative in his forties or fifties guiding her by the arm toward a waiting car.

When everyone had gone, Crane was still there. Standing. Staring. At the arrangements of flowers near the hole in the ground where Mary Beth was. And would be.

Boone was still back by the car. She called out to him.

"Are you about done?" she said. Cold as stone.

"Hey—fuck you. I can walk back to town."

"Suit yourself."

A few minutes later he realized she was standing beside him, now, and she said, "Look. You better come with me. Come on."

Crane rubbed some wetness away from his eyes and he and Boone walked to the Datsun.

"You got a place to crash?" she asked him.

"Motel."

"Leaving tonight?"

"I guess."

They got in the car and drove out of the cemetery.

"You'll be starting back to school, then," Boone said, suddenly, after several minutes of silence.

"Uh. Yeah. Sure. I guess."

"Fine. That's just dandy."

"What's your problem?"

"My problem?"

"You don't know me. I don't know you. But the hostility in here's so thick I'm choking."

"Yeah. Well. I shouldn't take it out on you."

"Take *what* out?"

"I liked Mary Beth. That's all."

"*I* loved her." His eyes were getting wet again.

22

"I'm sorry. Sorry, Crane. She never said a bad word about you. She loved you. She did."

They were at the motel now.

Crane got out.

"If she loved me," he said, "why'd she kill herself?"

"Who says she did?" Boone said.

And drove away.

4

Mary Beth's mother lived in one of the new houses in the development on the edge of town, a split-level that differed from the pale yellow house on its left and the pale pink house on its right by being pale green. There were a lot of cars parked in front of the place and in its driveway. Crane walked across the lawn, with its couple of sad-looking scrawny trees, and past a trio of men with their coats off and beers in hand, talking loud. He didn't hear Mary Beth's name mentioned in their conversation.

He knocked on the screen door (the front door stood open) and a middle-aged woman with a floral print dress and a haggard look greeted him with a suitably sad smile, saying, "We're so glad you stopped by." He had never seen her before.

He said, "Thank you," and was inside the living room with a dozen other people, who stood in small groups, talking in hushed voices, plates of food and cups of coffee in hand. All the chairs were taken. On the couch, flanked by elderly female relatives, was Mary Beth's mother. He went over to her.

It took her a moment to recognize him.

"This is Mary Beth's fiancé," she said, with a weak smile, nodding to the woman on her left and to her right.

They were all pleased to meet him and he took each offered hand and returned it.

He looked down at Mary Beth's mother and again saw Mary Beth's eyes in the plump face, and impulsively, leaned over and kissed her cheek. It surprised her. She touched her face where he'd kissed her and said, "There's food in the kitchen."

There was food in the kitchen. A table of it: hors d'oeuvre plates, plates of cold cuts, white bread, rye bread, nut bread, banana bread, chocolate chip cookies, sugar cookies, pecan pie, lemon meringue pie, angel food cake. Food. People were eating it.

There were more men than women in the kitchen. Though it was serve-yourself, a woman in an apron stood behind the table of food, offering help that was never needed. Another woman in an apron was doing dishes: apparently some of the mourners had eaten and run, or perhaps some people were onto a second plate. The men stood with beers in hand, talking softer than the men out on the lawn but louder than the people in the living room.

Crane took some coffee, sipped at it occasionally, leaned against a wall in the kitchen. No one spoke to him. The bits and pieces of conversation that drifted his way didn't include Mary Beth's name.

He wandered off, unnoticed, into the other part of the house, the upper level of the split-level.

He looked in at Mary Beth's room. It was a small room, four cold pale pink swirled plaster walls, a dresser with mirror, a chest of drawers, a double bed with a dark pink spread. There was a stuffed toy, a tiger, on the bed, a childhood keepsake she'd had with her in their apartment. Little else in the room suggested Mary Beth's personality. This summer was the only time in her life she'd lived in this room. Her mother and father had moved into this house after she'd left home for college. So this was not a room she'd lived in, really.

But there were some books on the chest of drawers: Kurt Vonnegut, some science fiction, a couple of nonfiction paperbacks on ecology and such.

And his picture, that stupid U of I senior picture, was framed on her dresser. And a couple snaps of them together were stuck in the mirror frame. He removed them. Put them in his billfold.

"That's stealing," a voice said.

He turned and saw a plump woman in her late twenties in jeans and sweater. Her hair was dark and long and she looked very much like Mary Beth, but with a wider face, which made her not quite as pretty.

"Hi Laurie," he said. He'd never met Mary Beth's sister before, but he felt he knew her.

"Hi there, Crane," she said, and smiled and came across the room and hugged him hard.

They looked at each other with wet eyes and then sat down on Mary Beth's bed. She took his hand in both of hers.

"I'm glad you're here," she said.

"I didn't see you at the funeral."

"I wasn't there, I had to stay with Brucie." She gestured toward the doorway.

"Brucie? Your husband?"

"No. You're thinking of Bruce. He was my husband. Emphasis on was. We split up."

"Mary Beth never mentioned . . ."

"It wasn't too long ago. Two months."

"Brucie is Bruce, Jr., then."

"Right. Ten months old yesterday."

"I'd love to see him."

"He's next door, in my room. I live here, you know."

"I didn't know."

"Since the divorce, I live here. I'm not surprised

Mary Beth didn't tell you about it, because it's all a little bit of a downer. And talking with you on the phone once a week, well, it was something she looked forward to. She didn't want to talk about depressing stuff, I'm sure."

"Depressing stuff. Just how depressed *was* she, Laurie? She never gave me any indication . . ."

"Like I said, your phone calls were a bright spot in her week. She didn't want to spoil 'em, I guess."

For a while Laurie sat silently and so did Crane; her hands felt cold around his.

"What happened, Laurie?" he asked her.

She looked at him with a face that was much too much like Mary Beth's and said, "I haven't the faintest idea."

"Laurie, Mary Beth wasn't depressed one day in the two years I knew her."

"She wasn't all that depressed this summer, either. Just kind of blue."

"Kind of blue."

"Worse, I guess, the last week or so."

"What happened the last week?"

"Crane, I was close to my sister, growing up. But we didn't talk much this summer. Something was bothering her, that much I know. What it was, exactly, I *don't* know."

"It had to be *something* . . ."

"Maybe you didn't know her as well as you thought. Never depressed a day while you knew her, huh? Well, a week after she got home I found her up in the middle of the night, sitting in the bathroom, bawling."

"What about?"

"I don't know. Her period, maybe, who can know? Only it was more often than that . . . I found her bawling like that four or five times."

"And she never said what was troubling her?"

27

"Once she admitted to me that she was thinking about Dad. He died of cancer about three years ago, you know. They were close. Being in this house reminded her of him, and that got to her."

"Got to her enough to make her do what she did, Laurie?"

"Who can say?"

"You mean you can understand it? You can understand somebody going into a bathroom and . . . and . . ."

"Slashing their wrists? I don't understand it, exactly. But I can see it. Haven't you ever thought about killing yourself, Crane? Hasn't everybody?"

"Maybe everybody else has. *I* haven't. It's a fucking waste, Laurie! It's the biggest fucking waste I can imagine."

"Why? Because life is so wonderful? What's wonderful about it?"

He pulled his hand away from hers. He didn't like what he was hearing coming out of this face that was so much like Mary Beth's. He didn't like the sickness that Laurie seemed to have, in a small way, that Mary Beth must've had in a larger way.

She must've sensed it, because she seemed to soften, reaching out and touching his shoulder as she said, "She loved you, Crane. I know she did. You were the most important thing in her life."

"A life that meant so little to her she flushed it down the goddamn toilet."

He stared at the wall. Laurie wasn't saying anything. When he looked over at her, she was crying into her hands.

"Laurie," he said, putting an arm around her, "it's been rough on you, too. I know that."

"I . . . I do know one thing that depressed her."

"Yes?"

"Brucie."

"Brucie?"

"Brucie. My little Brucie. She was unhappy for him."

He didn't understand that. He let it pass.

"Laurie, who found her?"

"Mom. In the morning. Mom came and got me up. Mary Beth had been gone for hours by the time we found her."

"Can I see where it was?"

"Sure," she said, shrugging.

She led him there.

He hesitated a moment.

Then he looked in and saw a bathroom, shining clean, guest towels hanging.

"I don't know what I expected," he said.

"I know," Laurie said. "It should be more dramatic than just a bathroom. But it's just a bathroom. It's the only one in the house, too, so both Mom and I were forced to use it, and that helped us, in a weird way. It helped make it just a bathroom. I use it sometimes and don't even think about her lying there."

He looked at Laurie. She was looking at the bathroom floor, blankly.

"Laurie," he said, guiding her back into the hallway. "Are you okay? I mean . . . are you really okay?"

"You mean, am I gonna be next?" She smiled a little. "I don't think so. I'm depressed. My sister just killed herself. I got a right to be. And, anyway, I got Brucie. I still got little Brucie. I live for that kid. You want to see him?"

"I sure do."

She took him into her room, a blue room with a bed with ruffled blue spread, and a Jenny Lind crib with a blue blanket nearby. She peeked in the crib and began playing with the well-behaved child, who made cooing, gurgling noises back at her.

Crane looked in at the child.

Brucie was adorable, but it wasn't hard to see why Mary Beth had been disturbed about the boy.

He didn't have any hands.

The street light on her block was out, but there were lights on in the downstairs of the big white two-story house. It was a gothic-looking structure with no porch and paint just beginning to peel. There were trees on either side of the place and the overall effect was rather gloomy. He knocked on the door.

He put his hands in his pockets and waited. It was a cool evening; perhaps he should've stopped back at the motel for his jacket. There was no sound except the crickets. No sound from within the house, either. He knocked again.

Finally a muffled voice behind the door, Boone's voice, said, "Who is it?"

And he felt another wave of embarrassment, like he had outside the church, after the funeral, and he couldn't bring himself to say anything. He turned to go.

He heard the door open behind him. Then: "Oh. It's you."

He turned and she was still in the plaid shirt and jeans, her blonde hair pinned back, pulled away from her face, and it was a good strong face with hard cheek-bones but very pretty. Her expression, though, was cold, condescending, and it pissed him off.

His face felt tight as he said, "What did you mean?"

"What?"

"What did you mean by saying Mary Beth didn't kill herself?"

"Did I say that?"

"You said it. And I want to know what you meant by it!"

"Is that why you were walking away with your butt tucked between your legs, when I opened the door?"

"Why don't you go fuck yourself."

"Why don't you just *go*? Go home, Crane!"

The door slammed shut.

He stood and looked at it, wondering what he was doing here, standing in front of this door, of this house, in this town, in this state . . . maybe going home wasn't such a bad idea.

But how could he, till he found out what Boone knew about Mary Beth's death?

He was raising his fist to knock again when the door opened. Boone leaned against the door and looked at his upraised fist, smirked, shook her head, sighed and said, "Come on in. You look like a horse's ass just standing there staring."

The house seemed very big inside, but that was because there wasn't much furniture, just a lot of dark wood trim and dark polished wood floors that reminded him of the church this afternoon; the cream-colored plaster walls and the secondhand-store furniture in the living room area she led him to reminded him of the duplex he used to share in Iowa City, where he and Mary Beth had spent their first evening.

She motioned to a sagging red sofa and he sat down. She pulled up a hardback chair, which was one of the few other pieces of furniture in the room. The place did look lived in; in one corner was a portable TV on a stand; against one wall was a small stereo flanked by speakers the size of cereal boxes, with a stack of albums, one of which — "No Nukes" — was propped up

32

against the wall; and in the middle of a floor covered by a worn braided rug was a red toy fire truck which clashed with the faded red of the sofa.

"My husband left me the house and the kid," Boone said, "and took all the furniture. Any other questions?"

"Jeez," Crane said, "it's kind of hard to picture you and some guy having trouble getting along."

"I had that coming," she said, smiling with almost no sarcasm at all. "Do you want something to drink?"

"Please. Nothing alcoholic."

"I got nothing alcoholic. You can have milk or herbal tea or juice."

"What kind of juice?"

"V-8 or orange."

"Orange."

She brought it to him, in a big glass with Bugs Bunny on it, with ice. She had V-8 and the Road Runner and no ice.

He sipped the juice and said, "Thank you."

She sat back down and said, "It won't kill me to be civil to you, I guess. For some reason I find myself wanting to take it out on you."

"Mary Beth dying, you mean."

"Yeah. That and my divorce and life in general. You just make a handy whipping boy."

"It's nice to serve a purpose."

"How did you find me? I'm not in the phone book."

"Laurie gave me your address. I just came from there."

"How are Laurie and her mother doing?"

"The mother seems dazed, in shock. People are standing around eating and smoking and talking about sports. How Laurie's doing, I don't know."

"Laurie has her problems."

"I know. I saw her son."

"Little Brucie isn't unique, you know."

33

"What do you mean?"

"Birth defects are nothing to write Ripley about, is what I mean. Especially around here."

"How so?"

"I know of two other women in Greenwood in the past three years whose kids were born with deformities. Mary Beth knew about them."

"Boone, I was down this road with Laurie . . . she seems to think Mary Beth was depressed over Brucie's birth defect, and by her father's death . . . but I just can't buy it. *You* knew her. Did she seem at all suicidal to you?"

"No. I told you . . . I don't believe she killed herself."

"What *do* you believe?"

"I believe she's dead. Don't you?"

He stood; the orange juice in his hand splashed.

"Goddamnit," he said, feeling red in the face, flustered, "*tell* me! Quit playing with me! If you know something, suspect something, let me in on the goddamn fucking secret!"

A little boy about six in a T-shirt and pajama bottoms wandered in. He had thick dark hair and was rubbing his eyes and saying, "Mommy, what's going on out here? I'm sleeping."

Boone smiled at the boy, trousled his hair and said, "Mommy's got company. Go on back to bed."

The boy looked at Crane and said, "Who are you?"

Crane didn't know what to say; he was standing there with a glass of orange juice in his hand, half of which he'd just splashed on himself, knowing he looked like an idiot, both to this six year old and himself.

"Just a friend of Mommy's," Boone said.

"If he stays all night I'll tell Daddy," the boy said.

"He won't be staying all night," she said, getting firm. "Now go to bed!"

34

The kid shrugged and said, "Okay," and gave Crane a dirty look and shuffled off.

Crane sat down. "Sorry I got loud," he said.

"I'm sorry I seem so evasive . . ."

"You've got a nice-looking boy, there."

"He looks like his father. Same disposition, too, I'm afraid."

"His father must be a good-looking guy."

"He is."

"There isn't much affection in your voice."

"There isn't much affection in me, period, where Patrick is concerned."

"Patrick? Your husband's name is Patrick Boone? *Pat* Boone?"

She smiled. "Yeah. We used to kid him about that, back in the old days." She laughed softly. "The old days. Did you ever think the Vietnam years would be the 'old days'?"

"Nobody ever thinks any time is going to be the 'old days.' That's when you met your husband, then? In college?"

"Yeah. He was a little older than me. We worked together on an underground paper. The Third Eye, it was called."

"Was that around here someplace?"

"No. Back in your neck of the woods — the Midwest. Eastern Illinois University. Very straight school. We were regular outlaws."

"It must've been a good time to be an outlaw."

"Yeah, I keep forgetting. You weren't there. You were just a kid. Still are."

"You're not that much older than me."

"I'm older than you'll ever be. You didn't even live through the draft, did you? Jesus."

"Neither did you. They weren't drafting women, the way I heard it."

"I lived through it with Patrick. A lot of young women lived through it with their men. Their husbands. Brothers. It wasn't easy for anybody with that hanging over them."

"You were active in the anti-war movement?"

"Yes. Patrick was. I was. We both were. Carried signs. We were at Chicago. Patrick got his head smashed by a cop. Pig, as we used to say. Six stitches. Back on campus, he was a draft counsellor. He was studying pre-law."

"So he's a lawyer now?"

"No. He shifted over into business and that's what he got his degree in." Her voice took on a sad sarcasm. "Currently he's in the personnel department at Kemco."

"Kemco. That's where Mary Beth was working this summer."

"Right. It's where her father worked. It's where everybody in this town who isn't a farmer works. Everybody in the whole area."

"Why do I get the feeling you don't like Kemco much?"

"I guess that's because it's what broke my marriage up."

"I see."

"No, I doubt if you do. What do you know about Kemco?"

"They're big. Not the biggest. But big."

"What do you know about Agent Orange?"

"Defoliant used in Vietnam. Some Vietnam vets exposed to it are now complaining about illnesses. Headaches, nausea, acne, that sort of thing. Lots of media play."

"Mary Beth *said* you were a journalism major. You really do know a little bit about what's going on in the world. Not much, but a little, anyway."

36

"Well why don't you bring me up to your level of awareness, then? If that's possible without dropping acid."

She flinched. "I said I was into the anti-war movement, way back when. I didn't say I did dope."

"Forget it. Go on." Crane wondered why dope was a sore point with Boone; but she was talking again . . .

"Agent Orange is an herbicide. We dumped forty-four million pounds of it on Vietnam. To kill the plants, so we could see the people better, to kill them, too."

"Don't take this wrong," Crane said, "but it *was* a war. Killing the enemy is the point in a war."

"The point is *that* undeclared war was supposed to be saving a country for democracy. Doesn't it strike you as odd that one of the ways we saved that country for democracy was to dump poison on it? Poison that killed plants, and animals, and people, and caused miscarriages and raised the infant mortality rates and . . ."

"And Kemco made this stuff?"

"One of the major suppliers, yes. I remember when they came to our campus in the early '70s, recruiting, and we protested. And nobody protested harder and louder and better than Patrick. Nobody."

"Only now he works for them. For Kemco."

"Right."

"He took the job and you divorced him."

"It wasn't like that."

"I'll tell you what it was like. He told you he'd work from within. Change the system by getting inside the system. That he'd cut his hair and put on a three-piece suit and be quietly subversive."

He'd struck another nerve: she got up and walked over to him and looked down at him with a stone face and said, "I didn't leave him, Crane. He left me. Because I wasn't the corporate wife. I didn't adjust to the life-style. I couldn't entertain his business associates. All I could do was spend my time writing my 'little articles,' as he called them, for what remains of the radical underground press."

She sat next to him.

"He bought this house, you know," she went on, "and filled it with modern furniture. Can you image? This house must be seventy, eighty years old — it's beautiful — and he fills it with modular this, and modular that. The son of a bitch. He sold me out. He sold us all out. Himself especially. That's the worst fucking part."

"People change."

"Oh, fine. People change. They drift apart. Like in, one of them stays in Iowa and digs ditches, and the other one comes home to New Jersey and slashes her wrists."

It hit him like a physical blow. She saw it and said, "Sorry. Sorry. I keep taking it out on you, don't I? Mary Beth didn't get depressed and kill herself, Crane. Kemco killed her."

"Yes, well," Crane said, rising. He handed her the half-empty glass of juice and said thanks.

"You're writing me off as a nut, aren't you?" Boone said, quietly, calmly, following him to the door.

"Good night, Boone," he said, and let himself out.

"You'll be back," she said from the doorway.

He'd have felt better about it if there had been some hysteria in her voice, when she said that; some bitter craziness.

But there wasn't.

"They killed her, Crane," she called out to him. Quiet. Sane.

He walked away from the house and crossed the quiet town and went to his motel room and tried to sleep.

38

Waking up came as a surprise to Crane: he didn't remember falling asleep and, for a moment, didn't know where he was. Then the yellow walls brought the motel back to him. He sat up in bed. He had a sense that he'd been dreaming, but he didn't remember what about. He did know that he was glad the dream was over.

He got up and showered and put on his jeans and a shirt and stuck his head out the front door. A brisk morning, but he wouldn't need a jacket. He glanced at his watch: ten minutes after ten. Had he slept *that* long?

He sat back down on the bed, feeling disoriented, off balance. He didn't feel so hot, his stomach grinding at him. Then he realized, suddenly, that he hadn't eaten yesterday.

He walked from the motel to the business district, five blocks of double-story white clapboards, an occasional church and the constant trees for which Greenwood had undoubtedly been named, a few of which were turning color as fall took hold. The business district took up a couple of intersecting streets and consisted of old buildings with new faces: hardware, florist, druggist, accountant, insurance, jewelry, medical clinic, pizza place, laundromat, one of everything, and two each of bars and cafes. An American flag drooped outside the Wooden Nickel Saloon, an old brick building painted white with a Pabst sign in the window; next door was a unisex hairstyling salon. Across the street was the Candy Shop Restaurant, a two-story brick building with a white wooden front and a green-and-black striped awning that said: "Since 1910." A neon sign, circa 1940, said candy in yellow, soda in red and lunch in yellow. He went in.

On the right was an old-fashioned soda fountain, with a mirror wall behind it upon which magic marker menus were written; on the left, a "penny candy" showcase — the penny candy starting at a nickel — and an oak cabinet displaying everything from sunglasses to aspirin. There was a high, white sculpted ceiling and walls that were dark wood and mirrors, with booths on either side of the long, narrow room, with porcelain counter tops and reddish brown leather seats.

Behind the soda fountain was a man about seventy with white hair and a white coat and wire-frame glasses who was probably called "Pop." Crane felt like Andy Hardy.

"Help you?" the man in white said, his voice high-pitched and forty or fifty years younger than him.

"Can I still get breakfast?"

"Sure. Take a booth and the girl will be with you."

None of the five seats at the counter was taken, but several of the booths were; there was a cop in one of them, drinking coffee and looking at a paper, a guy in his mid-twenties, thin, dark. Crane took a booth.

The person "Pop" had referred to as the "girl" turned out to be a friendly heavy-set woman about fifty. Did this make "Pop" sexist? It was a mystery to Crane. He ordered eggs and bacon and juice and got it quickly, ate it quickly.

Then he went over to the booth where the cop was sitting. The cop looked up from his paper and coffee with a smile, then realized he didn't know Crane and his expression turned neutral.

"My name's Crane. I'm from out of state."

The smile came back, tentatively. "Sit down, Crane. I bet I know who you are."

The cop had the first real New Jersey accent Crane had run into in Greenwood.

"You do?" Crane sat.

"Mary Beth's boyfriend. Here for the funeral."

"You knew Mary Beth?"

"Just to say hello to. My younger brother was in school with her. Beautiful girl. What a waste. I'm really very sorry, Crane."

Crane glanced at the front of the cop's uniform to see if his name was there.

The cop picked up on it, smiled again, said, "Name's Ray Turner."

They half rose in the booth and shook hands.

"I wonder if you could give me some information, Officer Turner."

"Ray. Sure, if I can."

"I'd like to talk with the officer who was called to the scene when Mary Beth's . . . when Mary Beth was found by her family."

"You *are* talking to him."

"Oh?"

"That's right. I handled that."

"I didn't expect to stop the first cop I saw and . . ."

"No big coincidence. We only have three full-time people on the force, Chief included. Plus a few part-timers."

"Must have your hands full."

"Not really," Turner said, sipping his coffee, smiling again. "We don't have a highway running through town, you know, so we don't use a radar car. What's the point of a speed trap, if you're off the beaten path? We do have schools to look after, morning, noon, afternoon. Run regular patrols at night, checking buildings and such. And accidents happen, now and then; we cover some of them out on the highway, if we're closer to it than the state patrol. Otherwise it's real quiet around here."

"So a suicide must be pretty unusual."

"Not really. We've had our crimes here. Bank was robbed, a year ago. We've had our murders. A few months ago a guy shot his wife and two kids and himself." Turner gazed into his coffee, distractedly. "'They' killed his wife."

"Pardon?"

"Nothing. Something the guy said before he blew his brains out."

"He said, what? That somebody else killed his wife?"

"*He* killed her, and his kids, too. Poor sad sorry son of a bitch. There was only one gun in the house and that's the one he used. 'They' were going to kill *him*, too. Typical paranoid nut."

"I see."

"That kind of thing doesn't happen everyday, Crane. I won't lie to you. This is a pretty soft job."

"Tell me about Mary Beth."

"I really didn't know her. Just to speak to."

"No. That morning. Tell me about that morning."

"Oh. Her mother called the station. That's over in the basement of City Hall. The Chief got the call. He called a local doctor, and the County Examiner. Informed the state patrol. Then we went over there. She'd cut her wrists, that you know. It was a little messy. The mother and sister were upset, so I asked

42

them their minister's name and they told me and I called him and he came over. The County Examiner was there within forty-five minutes. He pronounced her dead, of self-inflicted wounds, wrote it up in his book, and turned the body over to the family. I called the funeral home for 'em. They were upset, like I said."

"Right. So then there was no investigation?"

"Of what?"

"Her death!"

"I just told you. It was clear-cut. There's no doubt with a thing like that."

"I suppose you see suicides every day."

"Not every day," he said, smiling, without humor. "I been working here a year and a half and there's been four, five, including the guy I told you about. People get depressed. Life's a bitch, ain't you heard?"

"I heard. Look, I don't mean to be insulting, Officer Turner. Ray. But if you Greenwood cops act mostly as crossing guards and ride around checking buildings after dark, how can you be sure you're up to investigating what could be murder?"

"What the fuck are you talking about?"

"Mary Beth's death. How do you know it wasn't just supposed to look like a suicide?"

"What's that supposed to mean?"

"It's just . . . nobody really looked into it. It *could've* been something else, other than the way it looked. Can you deny that?"

"It was suicide."

"Why didn't the state patrol investigate it? What qualifies a glorified security guard to . . ."

"Hold it. Right there. First, we did call the state patrol, I told you that. We're supposed to do that, it's the procedure. If we think they should come in on it, or if they think they should come in on it, they come

43

in on it. But any cop worth a damn knows a clear-cut open-shut suicide when he sees it. Second, this wasn't my first job, pal. I worked in Newark for two years and got my fill of *real* police work. I didn't like it. So I came back to my hometown here and took this candy-ass job. But I *been* there. I *seen* murders. I *seen* suicides. This wasn't murder. It was suicide. I know what I'm talking about, here. I know what I'm doing."

"I didn't mean to imply you didn't."

"Sure you did. Glorified security guard my ass. You think we didn't talk to the family, the mother, the sister, to see if she had been depressed lately or not? They said she had. Why didn't *you* know that? You're the boyfriend. Didn't she write you or anything?"

"Nothing she wrote me or said on the phone indicated her state of mind was so . . ." He swallowed. "Look. Both Mary Beth's sister and mother were asleep when she died, which was in the middle of the night. Who's to say somebody didn't sneak in, maybe . . . what, chloroform Mary Beth and cut her wrists for her and . . . it sounds far-fetched, but couldn't it have been that way? Shouldn't you have checked to see if it happened like that?"

Turner looked at him for what seemed like a long time. "I know how you feel. What you're going through. You're looking for reasons, answers, and there aren't any. Life gets to people, sometimes. And sometimes they do something about it."

"I guess."

"Your girl killed herself. It begins and ends there. Let it go. Go home. Bury it."

Crane nodded, got up from the booth.

Walking out, he didn't feel much like Andy Hardy, anymore. Behind him he heard Turner call out to the "girl" for more coffee.

He walked back to the motel, stopping for a few

44

seconds to look at Boone's house. Some of the trees in her yard looked dead.

He packed.

He had one thing to do, before he left. Then he'd leave it behind him, like the cop had said. Leave it buried.

7

There were no cars in front of Mary Beth's mother's house, now, just a several-year-old Buick in the drive. The relatives, the mourners, had faded back into their own lives. Mary Beth's mother, her sister Laurie and little Brucie would be alone, now.

Laurie was coming out the front door as he was coming up the walk; she was digging her car keys out of a jacket pocket, and smiled when she saw Crane.

"Crane. How are you today?"

"I don't know. Okay, I guess. You?"

"Better. Not feeling so blue. You don't have to worry about me, if you were."

"Well it did seem like the strain had got to you a bit. But you'll do fine, Laurie. You and your kid'll do fine."

"I'm just going to get some groceries. There's plenty of cake and cookies and garbage left from yesterday, but no food. You can ride along, if you want to talk."

"Actually, I kind of wanted to chat with your mom. I haven't really had a chance to, yet. How is she?"

"Not bad. Existing. She hasn't said much, but it's her nature to be on the quiet side. Doctor has given her some mild sedatives, too."

"Would it be all right if I went in and talked with her?"

46

"I'm sure the company would do her good. She and Brucie are in the living room. Just go on in."

"Thanks, Laurie."

"I'll see you later, then."

"Well. Maybe not."

"Oh?"

"Yeah. I'll be leaving this afternoon. That's why I wanted to make this call on your mom, actually."

She gave him a long look and smiled as she did; it was a very good-natured, and very sad, smile. Her plumpness and wide face did not diminish the strong resemblance to Mary Beth. It made him want to be around her and at the same time not.

She kissed his cheek.

"Good-bye, Crane," she said, and turned and walked to the Buick.

Laurie had said to go on in, but he knocked anyway, and a soft, childlike voice from within said, "Come in, please."

He went in.

Mary Beth's mother was sitting on the couch, just as she had the day before, after the funeral, when she'd sat framed by relatives. It was as though she hadn't moved since. Brucie was nearby, where she could watch, her hand on the edge of his playpen, barely moving, a photorealistic sculpture.

Her head turned slowly on her neck as she looked at Crane; her movements reflected the sedation she was on—she moved like Lincoln at Disneyland: vaguely human, but not terribly convincing.

But she did manage a slow, small smile, recognizing Crane immediately this time.

"Nice to see you, young man," she said. It was a voice you could barely hear.

He went over and sat beside her.

"I'm going to be leaving this afternoon," he said.

47

"And I wanted to stop by and say good-bye."

"Kind of you," she said. She was still smiling; the smile hung there on an otherwise blank face.

"I wish you and I could have gotten to know each other better."

"Yes," she said, but there was confusion in her face, now, and in her voice; she really had no idea why Crane wished he could have known her better.

So he told her: "I loved Mary Beth. Very much. We'd have been married soon."

"I know," the mother nodded, with her blank smile.

"And we'd have been family, you and me. I'm sorry that didn't happen."

Somewhere beneath the sedation, what Crane was saying began to sink in. The smile became less mechanical, Mary Beth's eyes looked out of her mother's face at him.

Then he was crying, and she was comforting him. Holding him.

"I'm sorry," he said, pulling away gently. "Sorry."

"I know," she said. "Can I ask you something, young man?"

"Anything."

"Why?"

"Pardon?"

"Why did my little girl die?"

The question surprised him: he had no answer.

She said, "You knew her so well. Can you tell me why?"

"I can't," he said, finally. "I hoped I might find the answer here in Greenwood. But I don't think I can. I hoped your daughter Laurie might've been able to tell me, but she couldn't."

"You hoped I might tell you, too, didn't you?"

"Yes," he said, confessing to her and to himself, without saying so, that he'd come here today not to

48

say good-bye really, but for one last try at finding the answer to the question that Mary Beth's mother was now asking him.

"You lived with her this summer," Crane said, looking into the sedated face and hoping to keep the person behind it in touch with him. "Did you know Mary Beth was depressed? Troubled? Laurie says there were some indications she was."

The mother thought about that for a few moments. "She seemed a little down," she said, gazing at the floor. "She talked about her father a lot. She said, two of her best friends in town, their fathers died of cancer, too. She said that more than once."

"I see."

The woman looked over toward Brucie and gestured slowly. "She was upset about Brucie's problem. That made her unhappy. Sometimes she cried about it."

"She never told me," Crane said. "We spoke on the phone every week, exchanged our letters, but not a word about any of this."

"I can tell you one thing," the mother said, touching Crane's arm, her smile anything but mechanical now, "she was never down after your phone calls. She was never down after your letters. She loved you."

Crane held the tears back. "It's hard to understand how she could love me and take away the one thing that was most precious to me: her."

She touched his face. "She was sick. Like her father was sick. Just a different kind of sick."

He hugged her. She hugged back. She was soft. He could've stayed in her arms forever; it was as close to Mary Beth as he could get, now.

He rose. Smiled, said, "I'd like to keep in touch."

"That would be nice."

"I have your address. Do you have mine?"

"Yes. Send a card at Christmas."

"I will. You, too."

"Would you like to hold Brucie before you go?"

"Uh, no. I wouldn't want to disturb him."

"He isn't sleeping. Hold him for a while."

She got up, moving like a film slowed just slightly down, and gave the bundled baby to Crane. He held Brucie. Looked at him. He was a beautiful baby. Happy. Look Ma. No hands.

He handed Brucie back to her and she took him in her arms and rocked him.

"Well," Crane said. "I better say good-bye."

"Good-bye, son."

Back in the motel room, he sat on the bed and called to find out about the bus and the plane he'd be connecting with. Then he called his friend Roger Beatty, back in Iowa City, to let him know he was coming home.

"I'll be waiting at the airport for you," Roger said. "It'll be good to have you back. There's nobody here to go to lousy movies with me."

He and Roger often went to the Bijou, which was a theater within the Student Union where old films were shown.

"I'll be glad to be back," Crane admitted. "This hasn't been pleasant."

"I can imagine. How's her family? It's just her mom and her sister, isn't it?"

"Yeah. They're doing pretty good, considering."

"And how are you doing? Pretty good, considering?"

"I guess. I . . . well, I hoped to come away from here feeling I understood why this happened. But I don't, really."

"You're going to drive yourself crazy looking for a reason, Crane. You know what Judy said?"

Judy was Roger's girlfriend, a science major, Ph.D. candidate.

"No. What did Judy say?"

"She said one theory, which is I guess widely accepted these days, is depression comes not just from events in your life that get to you, but a biochemical breakdown in brain function."

"Jesus that's comforting, Roger."

"No. I'm just saying that you want an answer. You want to find out, what? That she found out from her doctor that she had a month to live, so she killed herself. That's the movies, Crane. I'm saying that, according to Judy at least, depression is a physical thing, not just a reaction to shitty things happening around you."

"I see your point. Look, this is costing me more money than my ticket back. I better get off the phone."

"Okay. But you don't sound so good."

"Well, fuck, what do you expect?"

"Get your butt home, Crane. Get home and forget about all this."

"I will, but it's just . . . there's this girl. Woman."

"Oh, really?"

"Give me a break, Roger. Her name is Boone. She was a friend of Mary Beth's. She's a fruitcake, is what she is."

"What about her?"

"She told me something crazy."

"Which was?"

"She told me Mary Beth was murdered."

"What?"

"You heard me. She's one of these leftist conspiracy nuts who thinks that the chemical plant everybody around here works for was behind Mary Beth's death."

"How so?"

"We didn't really get into it. She's just a flake, Roger. It wasn't worth listening to, really."

"Well it must be worth talking about, 'cause you're doing it long distance."

"It's nothing. I talked to the local cop here who handled it, and he said it was a clear-cut, cut-and-dry case."

"Really? How many suicides does a small-town cop like that handle, anyway?"

"More than you'd think. He said he's handled five in a little over a year."

"He said that?"

"Yeah. So what?"

"Oh. Nothing probably. Listen, what time should I be at the airport?"

"You were going to make a point, Roger. Make it."

"Oh it's nothing. Uh, tell me. What's the population of that town? What's it called? Greenburg?"

"Greenwood. 6000."

"I see."

"Roger."

"Crane, it's no big deal. It's just that five suicides out of 6000 people is a high suicide rate. I mean, I'm a sociologist. I know these things."

"You're a grad student. You don't know shit. How high a suicide rate is that, exactly?"

"About ten times the national average."

"I thought you'd be back," Boone said. "But I didn't think you'd bring your suitcase."

She was standing in the doorway with her arms folded, properly smug.

"It looks like I might be around for a few more days," Crane said. "I can't afford the motel much longer. Can you put me up?"

"I can put you up," Boone said, not budging in the doorway. "The question is, can I put up with you?"

"Right. I'll just go back to the motel and stay till my money runs out." He turned to go.

She put a hand on his shoulder. "You needn't pout. Come on in."

She led him upstairs, took him into one of the rooms, a big, completely empty one—nothing but smooth white walls and dark wood trim and polished light wood floor.

"I told you my ex took all the furniture," she said, shrugging. "The only two beds in the place are mine and Billy's."

"I can guess how your son would feel about sharing a bed with me."

"Right. About the same way I would."

"That's not what I'm here for."

"I know you're not. That wasn't fair. I have a sleep-

55

ing bag you can use, and there's a desk in Billy's room with a chair, which we can bring in and make this nice and homey."

"Thanks."

He followed her across the hall to a small room with a window and a big metal desk and not much else. To one side of the desk was a two-drawer gray steel file; on the other a couple wastebaskets. On the desk was a manual typewriter, around which were scattered notecards, tape cassettes, pages of rough draft and pages of manuscript. Above the desk was a bulletin board with newspaper and magazine articles pinned to it: "DO 'AGENT ORANGE' HERBICIDES DESTROY PEOPLE AS WELL AS PLANTS? THE EVIDENCE MOUNTS," "THE POISONING OF AMERICA," "KEMCO PROFITS UP."

"To which you no doubt say, 'Up Kemco Profits,'" Crane said, looking back at her archly, where she stood watching him take all this in.

"You will, too, once you hear the story," she said.

Crane poked around her desk a bit, just tentatively, waiting for her to stop him. She didn't.

"You can't be working on just an article," Crane said. "There's too much here for that. Is this the manuscript, so far?" He hefted the box of typescript. "There's a couple hundred pages, here."

"It's a book," she said.

"How long you been working on it?"

"Since Patrick and I split. Year and a half."

"Is it for a publisher? Do you have an advance?"

"It's on spec. I won't have any trouble selling it."

"How do you live?"

"Alimony. Child support."

"From Patrick? Who gets his money from Kemco?"

"I see it as ironic."

"I see it as hypocritical."

56

"Fine, coming from somebody who's freeloading in the first place."

"Yeah, well, you're right. That was uncalled for. Sorry. You wouldn't happen to have some coffee or something?"

"Herbal tea."

"That'd be fine. Can we go someplace where there's furniture? I'd like us to sit and talk, awhile."

"Sure."

Downstairs, he returned to the faded red sofa of the evening before, and she brought hot tea for them both, and sat next to him.

"Why did you come back, Crane? Why are you staying?"

"Because I don't think Mary Beth committed suicide. That's been my instinct from day one. And now I've learned something that convinced me."

"I suppose you found out about the other suicides."

"You mean you *knew*?"

"Of course. If you hadn't been so quick to classify me as a loon, I'd have been able to tell you that by now. I've been doing research into Kemco for a long time, Crane. I know a lot of things that you don't."

"What do the suicides have to do with Kemco?"

"All five suicide victims were Kemco employees."

"Jesus."

"Of course that could just be a coincidence. A lot of people around here work for Kemco."

"Jesus. Maybe they did kill her . . ."

"Where have I heard that before?"

"*Why* would they do it, Boone?"

"I don't know exactly. I may know. But I can't be sure."

"Tell me what you *do* know."

"The book I'm doing . . . it's called *Kemco: Poison*

and Profit . . . it mostly centers on what working at the Kemco plant near here has done to the residents of this and half a dozen other small towns, whose work force Kemco draws upon. What I've come up with is a pattern of miscarriages, birth defects and cancer, among Kemco employees and their children."

Crane sat and thought about that for a while.

"And Mary Beth knew about all this," he said.

"Of course. You know, I was in high school with Mary Beth's sister, Laurie, and Laurie and I were good friends back then, though we long since drifted apart. But even in those days Mary Beth was a sharp little kid — she was in grade school and way ahead of her age — and we used to talk. Then, this summer, we got together again and got kind of close. She was interested in my writing, my research, and I felt, considering how close she was to this, considering the tragedies in her own family, which related to the Kemco thing, it, well, seemed natural to let her in on it."

"No wonder she was depressed about her father . . . and little Brucie . . . she was seeing them as symbols of something larger . . ."

"It explains why she was blue, Crane, but it doesn't explain suicide. Because she didn't commit suicide. Not unless you believe it's possible for Greenwood to have ten times the national suicide rate."

"That's exactly what Roger said."

"Roger?"

"Friend back home. I called him, earlier this afternoon. When I told him there'd been five suicides here in a little over a year, he said that was about ten times the national average . . . without taking into account that rural areas have a 'markedly lower rate,' he said. Less pressure in the lives of 'rural residents' as compared to 'city dwellers.'"

"He talks like a sociologist."

"That's what he wants to be when he grows up."

"How about you, Crane? What do you want to be?"

"What do you mean?"

"You're supposed to be a journalism major. Why don't you dig in and help me with this goddamn thing."

"Your book? No. No thanks. That's not what I have in mind."

"I know it isn't. But you came here, to me, because you know we share a common purpose."

"I came here because you seem to know more about what's going on than the Greenwood cops do."

"The cops here are a joke. They're nothing."

"The guy I spoke to seemed competent enough."

"If they were competent, they wouldn't swallow these phony suicides whole."

"They're not all phony. One of them was a guy who shot his wife and kids — and then himself, in front of a cop."

"Fine. He's the one suicide Greenwood is statistically allowed. What about the other four?"

He looked at her. Nodded. Sipped his tea. It was still warm.

"Okay, then," he said. "You still have to explain some things. What was Mary Beth doing, where Kemco was concerned, that could've gotten her killed?"

"Maybe she stumbled onto something."

"What's that supposed to mean? What aren't you telling me?"

Boone got up and began walking around the braided rug, pacing, as she explained.

"You've got to understand," she said. "The book I'm doing deals with a lot of things. Agent Orange, for one. I've talked to dozens of Vietnam vets who came in contact with it, corresponded with another twenty or twenty-five. But I haven't come up with anything

59

new, really . . . much of what I have on Agent Orange is secondary source material. You're a journalism student, Crane, I don't have to tell you that firsthand, primary source material would carry more weight."

"I can see that," Crane said, keeping a calm tone. Trying to give her room to say what she wanted to say. "The story of Agent Orange would have a place in your book, but the book couldn't depend on that . . . it's a story that's been told elsewhere."

"Exactly! And the interviews, the statistics, laying out the pattern of illnesses here in Greenwood and other nearby small towns, whose populations largely consist of families supported by one or more Kemco employees, it's impressive, it's shocking even . . . but it's circumstantial. And, damnit, I'm no scientist. I can't say I've really proven *anything*."

"Can't you get inside the plant, to check on safety conditions and so forth?"

"Are you kidding? How, by asking Patrick, my ex-husband, for a tour? And what would I see on a company-directed tour? I'd get the standard P.R. shuffle, right? And suppose I got in on my own somehow, to really snoop around? What would I be looking for? How would *I* know how to judge the safety conditions in a chemical processing plant?"

"What you're saying is your book lacks something."

"It sure as hell does. I need a smoking gun, Crane."

"A smoking gun."

"Right! Something really tangible. Don't you get it? Don't you understand, Crane? Kemco is fucking *malignant*, festering, a bed of corruption and negligence . . ."

"I see," Crane said, hoping her journalistic style was somewhat more subdued.

"I need to be able to show Kemco being *criminally*

negligent. Not just a big well-meaning corporation that may have had some problems with plant safety."

"It doesn't sound to me like you have anything remotely like that."

"Oh but I do. In one of my interviews, with a company employee who was a friend of one of the 'suicide' victims, I learned that Kemco's playing dump-and-run."

"You've lost me."

"Kemco has to account to the federal government for the disposal of any potentially hazardous waste material; like this stuff PCB, which is used to insulate electrical transformers. Kemco makes that, and the waste from it can be dumped at only three federally approved sites. For years these companies dumped their shit wherever the hell they wanted . . . sewers, creeks, rivers. You know what they used to think? 'Dilution is the solution to pollution.' Only it didn't work out that way; there are plenty of toxic substances that *don't* harmlessly break down in water. So they started burying the stuff—Kemco, and Dow and Monsanto and DuPont and Hooker and all the others. Usually in 55-gallon steel drums, which eventually corroded and started to leak out into the ground, contaminating farmland and water supplies and people."

She was starting to rant; he tried to stop her: "Boone, I've heard of Love Canal. I know about things like that. But those are dump sites from twenty years ago. Things are more regulated than that now."

"In theory. You know, I'm glad you've heard of Love Canal, because so has Kemco, only they don't give a fuck. They are still hiring lowlife truckers to come dump this stuff God knows where, and with Christ knows what results on the environment and the people living nearby."

"What does any of this have to do with Mary Beth?"

61

"She was working this summer in Kemco's secretarial pool. A lot of the execs used her — she was good, and well liked; the daughter of a late, trusted employee. She heard some things. Saw some things."

"Such as?"

"One major thing, specifically: one evening, when she was working alone, staying late, trying to catch up on some work, she saw one of the executives give an envelope to a rough-looking guy who might've been a trucker. The trucker took some cash out of the envelope and counted it."

"That's it? That's what she saw? That's thin, Boone. That's goddamn thin."

"I don't think that's *all* she found out."

"Don't you *know*?"

"I was out of town for about three days, doing some research on the Agent Orange aspect of the book. When I got back, there were half a dozen messages for me to call her. I called. She was dead."

"She was snooping around for you, then. For your book."

"Crane, blaming me won't do any good."

"I'm not blaming you. Do you know the name of the exec she saw handing the money over?"

"Yes. It was Patrick."

From the highway, glancing over to the left, yellow-orange light stained the horizon, just above the trees. It was as if the sun were coming up at midnight. They turned off onto a blacktop and followed the signs that led them from one blacktop onto another, and another, and the stain against the sky became a city. A city of lights and smoke.

As the city's skyline emerged, the only skyscrapers were smokestacks, a dozen of them, emitting ever-expanding grayish white clouds that made seductive patterns as they rose.

Crane had expected the Kemco plant to be big, and it was; but it was more spread out, and closer to the ground, than he'd thought. There was an eerie, almost underwater look to it all, with the shifting smoke backdrop, the green-yellow-aqua outdoor lights strung about like bulbs at a particularly drab pool party. The taller, larger buildings resembled greenhouses, their walls sheets of mottled aqua-colored plastic, cross-hatched with metal, rising up amidst massive intertwines of steel pipe. There was a massive electrical substation nearby. Numerous one-story buildings. Countless chemical tanks. Off at the sides, huge, squat, silolike structures huddled like metal toadstools. Just inside a full-to-capacity parking lot, an American flag flapped against a grayish white breeze. The plant was going full throttle, but Crane had yet to see a human being.

Other than Boone, of course. She was driving. They were in her yellow Datsun. They passed a green tin building half a block long: the loading dock for Kemco trucks.

"That's where the trucks come out," Boone said, pointing as they approached a gravelled area to the left of the loading dock; a small brick building served as a clearing booth for departing trucks, of which there were none at the moment.

"Where do we watch from?" Crane asked.

"You'll see."

Opposite the Kemco plant, on the other side of the road they were driving down, was a flat open field; in the darkness it was hard to see how far the field extended. It resembled farmland. They'd passed several farms, within half a mile of the Kemco facility, on this same road; but this field wasn't being used for farming, or anything else, though perhaps it had once been a dump site for wastes—the proverbial "back forty" used by many chemical plants—long since filled up and smoothed over.

There was room alongside the road to park, which they did, a quarter of a mile down from the truck loading area.

"Are we going to be okay, here?" Crane asked.

"Sure. Nobody's going to think a thing about us."

"Yeah, right. What's conspicuous about sitting out here in the open like this?"

"It's dark. Nobody'll see us."

"A car going by will see us. A truck."

"Crane, one of the few nice things about the Kemco plant is it's out in the boonies . . . and you know what people in parked cars out in the boonies do, don't you?"

"I think I can guess, but I don't know what it has to do with us."

"If a car or a truck goes by, we pretend to be making out. Think you can handle that?"

"I suppose. But be gentle."

Boone frowned at that, but it wasn't a very convincing frown.

They sat and watched for an hour, saying very little, waiting for something to happen. Nothing did. The plant down the way, from this distance, looked like a cheap miniature in a '50s science-fiction movie. The longer he stared at it, the less real it seemed; yet at the same time, it struck him as being something breathing, something alive. It was the constant billowing smoke that did it, he figured.

Another uneventful half hour passed.

"I don't know about this," Crane said. "We haven't seen a car or truck since we got here."

"Crane, if we're patient, we can catch them in the act. You got that? We can wait and watch for the sons of bitches who are hauling Kemco's shit, follow them to wherever they're illegally dumping it . . ." She paused to point at the Nikon SLR camera on the floor between her feet. ". . . take a few nice candid shots, and we *got* them."

"And you're sure this is going to happen at night."

"It will *probably* be at night. They aren't called midnight haulers because they work days."

"It doesn't look like tonight's going to be the night."

"It's too early to tell. But tonight *might* be the night. Or tomorrow night, or the next night, maybe. This place turns out a lot of waste. We won't have to wait forever."

"That's encouraging."

"Take a nap. I'll wake you if anything happens."

"Don't let me sleep more than eight or ten hours."

"Crane, we only have to watch a couple hours a night. Between midnight and two, is all."

"I still don't know how you arrived at that."

"I guessed, okay? But they would probably wait till after third shift went on at 11:30, and, if they're going any distance at all to do the dumping, they wouldn't want to get started any later than two."

"I guess that makes sense."

"Take a nap."

"Okay."

Crane got as comfortable as he could in the Datsun, with her in the driver's seat. He was following her lead in this because he didn't know quite what else to do; she had the information, the insights, he needed. So he was going along with her on this effort to link Kemco with "midnight haulers." But it seemed to him ill-advised at best; and he didn't want to think about what it was at worst.

This afternoon, at Boone's, he'd listened to three cassette tapes — interviews with the wives of the three other suicide victims — and he'd found that, for a "journalist" who'd been working on a book for a year and a half, Boone had somewhat less than a professional interviewing style. She pushed her subjects, led them, tried to get them to help her make her preconceived points. (She had not interviewed any of the members of the Brock family — Mr. Brock being the man who killed his wife and two children and himself — as there was no one left to interview.)

Despite her lack of professionalism in interviewing, Boone was an amazing researcher and, from what he'd read so far, her writing style was considerably less hysterical than he'd supposed. Actually, it was a nicely understated style, getting her anti-Kemco points across convincingly. The Agent Orange section of the manuscript alone was devastating — her interviews with

Vietnam vets were much more effective than those with Greenwood residents — and she may have been wrong in assuming the book could not stand on Agent Orange alone to find her a publisher.

He was halfway through the manuscript and would finish it tomorrow; but he would need days to absorb Boone's file cabinet of data on Kemco's adverse effects on the citizens of Greenwood.

She had cooked supper for him, and it was delicious: lasagna, his favorite. They — Crane, Boone, Billy — ate in the kitchen, a big off-white room with plants lining the windows. Her husband had been nice enough to leave her all the appliances, but then most of them were built-in.

"This is really good," Crane told her, between bites.

"You sound surprised."

"It's just great. I hope you'll let me help out on the groceries, while I'm here. And I can do some of the cooking, if you like."

"You can cook?"

"Isn't that kind of a 'sexist' question?"

Boone smiled. "What's your specialty?"

"I'm glad you like Italian," he said. "I do terrific spaghetti and meatballs."

"Sounds wonderful. Only I'm a vegetarian."

"Really."

"You don't sound surprised."

"Well, I noticed the lasagna was meatless, of course, but, then I fix it that way myself. I like it with spinach and cottage cheese like this." He turned to the boy. "Are you vegetarian, Billy?"

"No!" the boy said. He was looking at his plate as he ate.

"I fix Billy hamburgers or tacos, when he wants," Boone explained. "I don't try to force vegetarianism on him. It's not a religion with me."

"Daddy feeds me steak," Billy said. Still looking at his plate.

"Daddy can afford steak," Boone told her son.

"How long are you going to live here?" Billy asked Crane, turning and looking at him for the first time. His expression was that of a prosecutor with an accused mass murderer on the stand.

"Just a little while, Billy," Crane said.

"Daddy won't like it," Billy said.

"Daddy won't know about it, either," Boone said.

"I might tell him."

"Not unless you don't want to live with mommy anymore."

"I might live with Daddy. If *he's* gonna live here, I might."

"Mr. Crane is my friend, Billy. He's helping me work. He won't be staying here long."

"He better not." Billy pushed away from the table. "Be excused?"

"Yes, Billy."

Billy left the table.

"He's a charmer," Crane said.

"He's not a bad kid. He doesn't like Patrick and me not living together."

"Well. No kid in his situation likes that."

"I don't think Billy's going to warm to you, Crane. You might as well get used to it."

"It doesn't bother me. I've lived with younger brothers. I can put up with it."

"Good. Thank you."

"Now that Billy's gone, there's something I need to ask about your husband."

"Yes?"

"How much does he know about this book you're doing?"

"Nothing, really. Patrick knows I'm writing a book,

68

but he's never bothered to ask what about. Which is fine with me. As far as I know, nobody at Kemco knows what I'm up to, exactly. And now that 'suicides' are becoming an epidemic around here, that's probably a good thing."

Earlier she'd told him that she had not yet confronted Patrick with what she knew Mary Beth had seen: that exchange of money between him and a questionable-looking trucker. Now looking across the kitchen table at her, in the house she'd lived in with her husband, Crane could see that as much as she disliked Patrick, as much as her hatred for Kemco was tied in with how she felt about him, she didn't like thinking Patrick might've been part of what happened to Mary Beth.

"This afternoon," Crane said, "I tried to absorb as much information as I could."

"I know."

"I'm just getting started, really. But already something is bothering me."

"What bothers you?"

"The 'suicide' victims. Okay, they all worked at Kemco. But otherwise I see no connection . . . we have a maintenance man, a foreman, an executive. Then there's Mary Beth — a secretary, temporary summer help."

"So?"

"It's just that the list is too disparate. It's not a group of people working together, in similar jobs, with similar access to information."

"They all worked at Kemco. That's connection enough."

"No it isn't. As you've said, *everybody* around here works at Kemco. What *other* connection did they have? Boone, I'm going to talk to the wives of those 'suicides' myself."

"Fine."

"Alone."

"That's fine, too."

"You see, I don't share your basic assumption that Kemco is evil. That all big business is the enemy of the people. I just don't buy that naive leftist bullshit, okay?"

"Please. I'm still eating."

"I just want you to understand that I'm in this only for one reason: Mary Beth. I want to know what really happened to her."

"That's easy. Kemco killed her."

"Kemco didn't kill her. Possibly some people that work for Kemco did."

"Kemco killed her. You're playing games with semantics, Crane."

"I'm *not* playing *any* kind of *game!*" He was standing. Angry.

"It hurts, doesn't it, Crane?"

"S-sorry," he said. Sitting back down.

"I know it hurts."

He felt words tumble out. "I dream about her. Every night. It's not the same, exact dream every night. But it's always Mary Beth, and she's alive, and we're together, and we're doing something, anything. Picnic, a play, at home listening to music and talking. Then I remember she's dead. Sometimes she touches my lips and shakes her head, smiling: 'Don't think about it,' she's saying. Sometimes she just disappears."

He was dreaming now. Mary Beth was sitting by him in a car.

"Crane," Boone was saying, "wake up."

He opened his eyes. Lights were coming down on them.

"It's a truck, schmuck," she said, crawling over on him, awkwardly.

70

They embraced.

The truck roared by; emblazoned on its side was KEMCO.

"One of their own," Boone said, still in his lap, looking back at the receding semi. "That's no midnight hauler. They're carrying product, not waste."

"Here comes another."

They kissed for a while, as half a dozen trucks rolled by; one truck honked, and they looked up, startled: a truck driver was smiling and waving at them.

When the trucks had passed, Boone got back over in the driver's seat and said, "We might as well call it a night."

"Right."

"They're not hauling any waste out of here tonight."

"Right."

Boone started the car, pulled onto the road. Crane felt uneasy, and a little ashamed, as he had back in the church, at Mary Beth's funeral, when he'd seen Boone and got an erection. Like the one he had now.

Boone seemed a little uneasy herself.

Behind them, Kemco, like a bad dream, faded. And lingered.

Harry Woll, a foreman at Kemco, had been dead just over a year. He'd taken an overdose of sleeping pills, washing it down with Scotch; that was the story. The house he'd lived in was two blocks from Boone's. Crane walked there.

It was another cool night. Crane wore his jacket, but it didn't keep his teeth from chattering. He supposed that was nerves, more than anything. He didn't like doing this. He couldn't have felt more uncomfortable.

Woll's house was one of several newer, one-story homes at the tail end of Woodlawn, a side street. There was a well-kept lawn with some shrubbery around the front of the pale green house, but there were no trees, which was unusual for Greenwood. The porch light was on.

Crane knocked on the front door.

A pretty redheaded girl of about fourteen, wearing snug jeans and a white T-shirt, answered. The T-shirt had a TWISTED SISTER logo on it; under it were pushy, precocious breasts that made the logo bulge. She looked at Crane and pretended to be sullen, calling out, "Mom! It's that guy who called."

The girl leaned against the door and a smile tugged at the corners of her pouty mouth. Crane gave her a noncommittal smile and looked away.

"Mr. Crane?"

Mrs. Woll was a slender, attractive woman about forty doing a good job of passing for being in her mid-thirties. She wore a light blue cardigan sweater over a pastel floral blouse and light blue slacks. Her hair was dark honey blonde and rather heavily sprayed. She had the face of a cheerleader or homecoming queen, twenty years later.

She extended a hand to him and gave him a dazzling smile. "It's nice to see you, Mr. Crane."

He managed to return her smile, but the warm reception threw him: why was she so pleased to see him? She'd never met him before.

He stepped inside.

"Take Mr. Crane's jacket, dear," she told her daughter.

The daughter took his jacket, brushing her breasts against him as she did, and tossed the jacket in a chair by the door.

"Would you like some coffee?" Mrs. Woll asked him, taking his arm, leading him to a sofa nearby, a painting of the crashing tide above it, one of several undistinguished oil paintings that hung in a living room of white pebble-plaster walls and contemporary furniture. The place was immaculate; either she was some housekeeper or had cleaned up because company was coming.

He said thanks, yes, to her offer of coffee and she left him to go get it. The fourteen-year-old redhead stood and looked at him and let her pout turn into a full-fledged smile and, butt twitching, walked into the next room, from which he soon heard a situation comedy and its laugh-track, TV turned up loud enough to be annoying on purpose.

Mrs. Woll brought Crane the coffee, smiled, and

went into the room where the fourteen year old had gone, and the TV sound went down. Some.

While this was going on, he glanced at the far end of the room, where a color studio photo of the Woll family, taken perhaps five years ago, hung above a spinet piano. In the picture, Mrs. Woll looked heavier, sadder; an older daughter, about fifteen in this picture, wore a lot of makeup and wasn't quite as pretty as the younger daughter (who was just a kid, here) was turning out to be. Mr. Woll was a jowly redheaded man, whose smile seemed forced even for a studio portrait.

Mrs. Woll came back and sat down next to Crane. "Now. You said you wanted to talk to me."

"It's very considerate of you to see me, Mrs. Woll. To agree to talk with me."

"Mr. Crane, I understand what you're going through, losing someone you love. If I can be of any help to you, in such a difficult time, I'm more than happy."

"Your husband's . . . death. Did it come as a shock to you?"

"My huband's *suicide*, Mr. Crane. It's important not to evade reality. You can use euphemisms, if you like, but I've found they're not really helpful. The sooner you face up to your fiancée's death as *suicide*, and deal with it honestly, the sooner you can get back about the business of *your* life."

"Yes. But did it come as a shock to you? By that I mean, did it happen out of left field, or was Mr. Woll suffering from depression in the weeks preceeding his . . . suicide?"

"I can't really say. My guess would be, yes, he was depressed."

"Your guess?"

"Mr. Woll and I were separated at the time of his

74

suicide. We might have gone on to get a divorce; it's hard to say."

"What was the problem, if you don't mind my asking?"

"His moods. He'd always been a moody individual, but it had gotten worse lately. At times, he even hit me. His daughters, as well. We have two girls, Jenifer you've met, Angie, who's nineteen, moved out and got her own apartment when she turned eighteen."

"Was that before or after Mr. Woll died?"

"Killed himself. Before. Harry couldn't handle the changes I was going through."

"Changes?"

"Mr. Crane, for nineteen years of marriage I worked, just like he worked. In fact, I brought in only a few dollars a month less than he did. But in addition to *my* job, I was supposed to be a full-time house-wife, as well—do all the cleaning, cooking, laundry. What extra effort did Harry make to help out around the house? Nothing. Not a thing. I put up with it for years. Years. Then finally I guess my consciousness got raised, like with a lot of women, and I put an end to it. I told Harry we could afford a cleaning woman. He blew up! But I hired her anyway. I told him he could either learn to cook, or start taking us out for meals. He laughed at that, but it didn't strike him so funny when he started coming home from work to no supper prepared, every other night. And so we started going out to eat a few nights each week. Our life-style changed—but Harry didn't, not really. I thought shar-ing the work load fifty-fifty was only fair, but he didn't see it that way. He said he was old-fashioned, like that explained it. And he drank, he drank too much. I tried to get him to enroll in AA, and that made him furi-ous. We had some very unpleasant months around here."

"I see."

"Harry and the girls weren't getting along too well, either. He and Angie were always going at it, because he felt she had loose morals. He accused Jenifer of the same thing, and she was only thirteen. Why, she's *still* a baby! Can you imagine?"

"No."

"So Harry took an apartment over the hardware store. That's where he took his pills and Scotch."

Crane sat there and tried to absorb what he'd just heard. Make some sense of it.

"Mrs. Woll, I need to ask you something that may seem a little . . . off the wall . . ."

"All right. Ask."

"Was there anything at all suspicious about Mr. Woll's death?"

"Suicide. No. I think he hoped someone would stop him. I don't think he really meant to do it."

"No, I suppose not. What I mean to say is, did you at the time — or do you now — have any suspicions, whether based on fact or just a feeling you might have, that Mr. Woll's death might have been something other than suicide?"

"I don't understand."

"Mrs. Woll, there have been five suicides in Greenwood in a little over one year. Mr. Woll was one; my fiancée, Mary Beth, was another. All five worked for Kemco."

"I still don't understand what you're driving at."

"Five suicides in a town the size of Greenwood is about ten times the national average. That strikes me as odd. And all five suicide victims worked for Kemco. That seems odd to me, too."

She smiled; she really was a beautiful woman. "*Now* I understand. Mr. Crane, accept your fiancée's death for what it was: suicide. It sounds harsh, but the truth

76

often does. Just because Harry and I were separated when he killed himself doesn't mean I'd stopped loving him. We weren't divorced, after all. We might've gotten back together. It was a crushing blow to me. I cried and cried. But I learned to accept it. Live with it. Life goes on."

"Uh, right. But that doesn't make the coincidences I mentioned any less odd."

"It also doesn't make them anything more than coincidences."

"Perhaps."

She touched his leg. "It's only natural that you find it hard to accept the fact that your fiancée took her own life. It's normal for you to try to make it be something else. Accept her suicide *as her suicide*, and not an accident or some conspiracy or other such nonsense — and get on with your *own* life." She leaned forward and, with a smile, lifted her hand from his leg and wagged a motherly finger at him. "Just because someone else threw their life away, doesn't mean you have to. More coffee?"

"No, no thanks."

"It's no trouble . . ."

"No, really," he said, rising. "Listen, it was really very nice of you to see me. Talk to me."

"My pleasure."

He moved toward the door. "Well, anyway, thank you. I know it must've seemed strange, getting a phone call from somebody you never heard of . . ."

"Don't be silly. I knew who you were."

"You did?"

"Of course. I knew Mary Beth. Isn't that why you came? Because you needed to talk to someone who'd known Mary Beth? Someone who'd been through what you're going through now, which I have, with my husband's suicide?"

77

"Uh, well. I didn't know how *well* you knew her."

"I didn't know her well, but I knew her. She was a wonderful person. It's a tragic loss."

"Did she talk to you about me?"

"Not really. She mentioned you. The girl was crazy about you, I'd judge. And I didn't blame her." She gave him an openly flirty look; her mouth was her daughter's. "I'd seen your picture, after all."

"She showed it to you?"

"No, it was on her desk."

"You *worked* with her?"

"Yes. I'm in charge of the secretarial pool at the Kemco plant. You knew that, certainly?"

"Uh. Certainly."

"Well, good night, Mr. Crane."

"Good night."

Just as the door was closing, the volume on the TV went up; he could hear the canned laughter.

The barrels were stacked four high, and everywhere. Toxic Tootsie Rolls, standing on end, more rows deep than Crane dared guess. In their midst was a sprawling warehouse, faded red brick with black windows, its loading-dock area clear, but otherwise surrounded by fifty-five-gallon barrels.

And the barrels looked sick. Piled haphazardly, unlabelled, many of them pockmarked, stained by unknown fluids that had streaked them like dried blood. Some of the bottom barrels were so corroded that weeds grew in and out of them, God knew how.

They'd taken the New Jersey Turnpike to Elizabeth, and Boone had guided the Datsun down this industrial waterfront stretch lined with storage tanks of gasoline and natural liquid gas that loomed like silver UFOs; the air hung with the smell of industry. At the end of this unshaded lane was Chemical Disposal Works, this Disneyland of waste drums they were now wandering around, like tourists, complete with camera.

"I thought you said you'd already been here," Crane said, uneasy that she was strolling around at two in the afternoon, and a sunny one at that, taking pictures of what had to be a criminal operation.

"Sure," Boone said. She was cheerful today, her long hair pulled back by a bright yellow headband, an incongruity next to her faded denim jacket and jeans and black-on-white NO NUKES sweatshirt. "But last time I was here they only had twenty thousand barrels. I'd say they're up to thirty, now."

"I mean, this *is* illegal, right?"

"I can take pictures here if I want. They don't have any no trespassing sign up, that I can see. We didn't climb a fence to get in."

"I'm not talking about that. I'm talking about this." He gestured to the barrels stacked on either side of the cinder drive they were walking along; the warehouse was up ahead, fifty yards.

She shrugged. "I contacted the Solid Waste Administration about it."

"And?"

"I was told this was a licensed facility."

"Jesus."

"I sent photos I took, and never heard anything. So I called back and was told Chemical Disposal Works had been 'administratively required' to clean up their site, within a 'reasonable amount of time.'"

"When was that?"

"Three months ago."

They had reached the warehouse. No one seemed to be around. Boone took pictures of the loading-dock area; there were no trucks present, however, just a battered-looking tan station wagon, which indicated perhaps someone was around. Crane was getting nervous.

"What's in those things, anyway?" Crane asked.

"The barrels? Who knows. Could be anything. Solvents. Plasticizers. Nitric acid. Cyanide. Pesticides. You know."

"That sounds . . . dangerous."

"You might say that. If they got certain compounds in 'em, exposure to the air could explode them."

"Explode."

"It's happened before. Not here, but it's happened."

"Does Kemco use this place?"

"I don't know. I just know I wanted you to see this place. It's not the only one of its kind, you know."

"I'm convinced," he said. "It's a real eyesore. Can we leave?"

"In a minute."

She was still at it with the Nikon.

Despite the sun, it was chilly. Crane buried his hands in his jacket pockets. The air here had a funny smell; not like the acrid industrial odor he'd noticed earlier, but something not unlike an unpleasant perfume, and reminiscent at the same time of rubber.

To the left of the loading dock a door opened. A short, stocky man in a blue quilted work jacket and brown slacks leaned out. He had a pale face in which thick black streaks that were eyebrows obscured all else.

He yelled at them: "Hey! What's the fuckin' idea?"

Boone stopped taking pictures and gave the man, who was about ten feet away, a bigger smile than she'd given Crane so far and said, "We're taking some pictures for our school paper. We're trying for a mood, here, you know?"

The eyes below the bushy black streaks narrowed: the guy didn't seem to be buying Boone as a teenager. It seemed a little lame to Crane, too, actually, but he didn't figure at this point he had much choice but to go along with it.

He moved toward the man, who was still in the doorway, and got between Boone and the guy, blocking her from view—Crane figured he had a better chance of passing for a school kid than she did—and

81

said, "We're going for contrasts, like, uh, things that'll look neat in black and white."

"Horseshit," the man said, and moved forward, brushing Crane aside, and pointing a finger at Boone like a pissed-off father. He stopped in front of her, his finger almost touching her nose.

"I remember you," he said. "You were around here last summer asking question. Taking pictures. Right before the state came down on our butts."

Boone kept smiling, but the manner of it changed.

The guy returned her smile, but his was as heavy with sarcasm as hers. "Honey," he said, "it's been many moons since *you* were a teenager."

"Go fuck yourself," Boone told him.

The guy didn't take that well. He grunted, and reached at the camera with one hand, latching onto one of her arms with the other, and squeezed. Boone yelped. But she didn't let loose of the camera.

Crane grabbed the guy by a depressingly solid bicep and tugged, but the guy didn't give any ground.

"Let her alone," Crane said, still tugging, still getting nowhere. "Let her alone, will you? We're leaving now, all right?"

The guy turned away from Boone, though he still held her by the arm, and said, with a spray of bad breath that almost matched the rubbery perfume of the air around them, "You're goddamn fucking well told you're leaving, but the film in that fucking camera isn't," and he ripped the camera out of her hands, opened the back of it and tore the film out, and flung the film against a nearby wall of barrels.

Then he handed the camera back to Boone and smiled and nodded and Boone swung a small fist at his face and connected, leaving the man's mouth bloody, the red looking garish in his pale face. He pushed her face with the heel of his hand, like Cag-

82

ney in the old movie, but minus the grapefruit.

Boone was on the ground, but she wasn't hurt; she was sitting there swearing up at the guy, who was laughing at her, sort of gently, and Crane swung a fist into the man's stomach, and surprisingly, doubled him over.

If they had run for it, then, it might have been over, but Crane got greedy. He took another swing, toward the guy's face this time, and the guy batted it away, even while doubled over, and then came out swinging himself, first into Crane's stomach, then into the side of his face, and Crane was unconscious for a while.

When he woke up, a minute or so later, Boone was cradling his head in her lap, sitting on the cinders, saying, "Crane? Crane?"

"Is he gone?"

"He went inside."

"Good. Can we go now?"

"Yes."

"He didn't break your camera did he?"

"No. The film is good and exposed, though. Did he break anything of yours?"

"My self-esteem. Otherwise, I'm fine."

"You're going to have a nasty bruise."

"No kidding."

She helped him up; he felt a little dizzy. She went and got her camera off the ground while he tried to stay on his feet. Then she walked him toward the Datsun.

"Go fuck yourself," Crane said.

"What?"

"That's what you told that guy. I can't believe you sometimes."

"I guess I do lack tact," Boone admitted. "Are you starting to understand?"

They were at the car.

"Understand what?"

She opened the door on the rider's side. "The seriousness of this."

He touched the side of his face. "I understand pain, if that's what you mean." He got in the car. She went around the driver's side and got in.

"I also understand why that guy was pissed off at us," Crane said. "Like anybody in his place would be."

"You can rationalize anything, can't you, Crane? Even getting the shit beat out of you."

She started the car. Crane looked back at the barrels, standing on top of each other, as if to get a better look at them as they drove away.

They were parked alongside the road again. The midnight skyline of the Kemco plant was a study in plastic and steel and soft-focus green-yellow-aqua light, against a backdrop of smoke and smokestacks.

"Why doesn't it make any noise?" Crane asked. "It's creepy that it doesn't make any noise."

"It isn't a noisy operation," Boone shrugged. She was leaned back casually in the Datsun's driver's seat, munching on sunflower seeds. The near-darkness they were sitting in made for interesting shadows on her face; she looked quite lovely, for a girl, woman, eating sunflower seeds.

"What are they making in there, anyway?" he asked her.

"Herbicides. Pesticides. Plastics. Lots of things."

"Useful things," he countered.

"Right. Like Agent Orange."

"Are they still making that?"

"Yes, and PCB, until a year ago."

"Isn't that a little unfair?"

"Bringing up the recent past? I don't think so. I don't think there should be a statute of limitations, just because the murder you committed was ten years ago."

Crane said nothing.

"I don't object to everything they make. I know a

lot of farmers depend on the stuff . . . though personally I can't see eating anything that isn't organically grown."

"Jeez, who'd have guessed?"

"What's with you, Crane?"

"What do you mean?"

"You're really on the rag tonight."

"I guess I am. Sorry."

They sat. Boone ate her sunflower seeds, watched the loading-dock area. It seemed a quiet night: not a Kemco truck to be seen. Crane was still studying the Kemco plant itself, fighting ambivalent feelings. His face hurt, from where he'd been hit.

"What are those things?" he asked her, pointing.

"Those fat silo things? Storage vats."

"What's in them?"

"Waste, I guess."

"They're fucking huge."

"That they are."

"You can't be right. There isn't that much waste coming out of this one plant."

"You been reading my research material, Crane. You're up on how much hazardous waste is produced in this country every year."

Yes he was. Thirty-two million tons. But somehow it seemed obnoxious of her to mention it right now.

"I also know," Crane said, "that this plant, like most chemical processing plants, has its own waste-disposal unit. They are *not* dumping all that shit illegally."

"Of course they aren't. Most of it gets dumped in the river."

"What river?"

"The Delaware River."

"Where's that?"

She pointed back behind the Kemco plant. "We can

drive straight into it, if you like . . . we aren't a mile from it."

Feeling foolish, he said, "The stuff's processed when it goes in, isn't it? It's probably cleaner than the river it's going into."

"Maybe. But that's not what we're here for. We're here to find out about the stuff they *can't* run through their disposal unit. The stuff they have to dump."

"Yeah. Okay."

"Something's wrong, isn't it, Crane?"

"No. Yes. I'm just . . . trying not to get caught up in your . . . crusade. It's dangerous, what you're doing. It's not what a journalist does."

"What does a journalist do?"

"You keep an open mind when you look into something. You don't set out to prove something. You set out to find the facts, whatever they are."

"Yes, and your problem is you can't face facts, when you find 'em."

"No! My problem is keeping myself reminded, in the midst of your leftist hysteria, that there are two sides to everything. Even to Kemco."

"It's that talk you had with Mrs. Woll, isn't it? That's what's bothering you."

"No."

"I think we should talk about that."

"I told you what she told me."

"But you can't handle it, can you?"

The windshield was fogged up from their talking; that was okay, because if anyone drove by, it would reinforce the idea that he and Boone were making out. Which was hardly the case at the moment. He turned to her. Calm. Rational.

He said, "Mrs. Woll opened up to me, a little bit, possibly because I'm male, and also because I know

87

how to interview better than you. But for the most part, she didn't say anything that wasn't on the tape of your conversation with her, a year ago."

"There was the news that she worked with Mary Beth at Kemco."

"News to *me*. You knew about it, 'cause Mary Beth would've told you. You just wanted me to find out for myself."

"Maybe," she smiled. "When I interviewed her originally, not long after her husband's 'suicide,' she was a secretary at City Hall. Had been for some years. Since then, she's been given a, shall we say, enviable position at Kemco. Head of the secretarial pool, no less."

"And into that, I suppose, you read all kinds of conspiratorial under- and overtones. Tell me, did Kemco kill Kennedy?"

"Which one?"

"Boone, Kemco offering an employee's widow a position with the company could be a strictly benevolent act on their part. It isn't necessarily anything sinister."

"She was qualified for the job, I grant you. But surely you find it slightly suspicious . . ."

Crane looked away from her. Said nothing.

"Of course you do," Boone said. "That's what's bothering you. Isn't it?"

He sighed, shook his head. Turned and looked at her.

"Yes," he admitted. "That, and that we've made a connection between Mary Beth and one of the other 'suicide' victims. An indirect connection, but a connection."

Boone nodded. "She's connected to another victim, too: Paul Meyer. He was an exec, and Mary Beth was the darling of the secretarial pool, where the execs were concerned."

"Which could explain how she stumbled onto some high-level shenanigans. Well. Anyway, I'll be talking to Meyer's wife tomorrow; we might get some insights, there. This is all very flimsy, from an evidence stand-point, you know."

"Maybe. But maybe we should both try to keep an open mind."

"Yeah. Maybe you're right."

"A truck."

"Huh?"

"That could be a truck."

Light caught the corner of Crane's eye and he turned. Down the road, about a mile, were the high-beams of what appeared to be a truck, approaching Kemco.

"Get in the back seat," Boone told him.

He did. She passed the Nikon to him.

The truck—it *was* a truck—came into view. It was a big flatbed with the sides built up; a tarp was flung over the back of it, tied on. This they saw as it pulled into the gravelled loading area.

"Did you notice the clearing booth was empty to-night?" Boone asked him.

Crane, in the back seat, feeling nervous, said, "No I didn't."

"Well it was."

"That isn't one of Kemco's trucks, is it."

"It sure isn't," Boone said. She was smiling. "It's an independent. Come to pick something up."

89

Boone drove by the loading-dock area at about twenty-five miles an hour. Crane, out the back window of the Datsun, took half a dozen pictures of the flatbed truck, which was waiting near the big green tin shed while one of the two men in its cab, a burly guy in a thermal jacket, hopped out to talk to a Kemco hard hat, who was gesturing, giving instructions for where the truck was to go to pick up its load.

The Kemco plant receded behind them.

Boone looked at him in the rear view mirror. "How did you do?"

"I'm not sure," he said, crawling back up in front, giving her the camera as she drove. "I hope there was enough light."

"You had it wide open, didn't you? There was plenty of available light. I'm sure they'll come out."

Crane hoped so. It was a clear night, with stars and a moon; that and the lights of Kemco itself should've made for some good shots.

"What now?" he asked.

"Wait half an hour and go back."

She pulled over to the side again; they were about a mile down from Kemco, now. She turned the motor off.

"Don't we have enough already?" Crane asked.

"You're kidding. We're just getting started."

90

"If you say so."

"Are you nervous?"

"Of course I'm nervous. I'm scared shitless. Aren't you?"

"Somewhat. There's really nothing to worry about."

"You must not've seen the three-hundred-pound trucker that climbed out of that rig."

"Nobody spotted us. Nobody's going to spot us."

"Next on the program, I suppose, is some shots of the truck pulling out of Kemco, loaded up."

"Right."

"Surely we're not just going to go tap dancing by again, are we?"

"No. We'll pull into their parking lot. We can get some good shots from there and we won't be noticed. I've got a zoom lens in the glove compartment. I'll take the next shots. You drive."

"All right. We might as well switch places now."

He got out of the car and walked around to her side. The night air felt chill but he rather liked it; it was like splashing his face with water in the morning to wake up—it reminded him he was still alive. He opened the car door for her and she got out.

They stood there for a while, leaning against the front of the car, enjoying the stillness, their backs to Kemco, looking out at the night. Pale ivory moonlight bathed the farmland around them with a quiet beauty. It didn't look so bad on Boone, either.

Half an hour was up.

Crane drove back to Kemco, pulling into the parking lot, which was, as it had been last night, nearly full; but they found a place, and from it they could see the American flag, which Kemco flew twenty-four hours a day, and, just across the way, the loading-dock area. The truck was nowhere to be seen.

"Did we miss it?" Crane asked her.

"I don't think so."

"Couldn't it have pulled out and gone down the other direction?"

"Possibly. If so, it wasn't loaded up; hasn't been time for that."

"Where is it, then?"

"Somewhere on the Kemco grounds picking up its cargo. My guess is they didn't want to store the stuff in their normal loading area. What they're doing here isn't something they want to advertise, you know, not even to their own employees."

They sat and watched.

Boone opened the glove compartment and got the zoom lens out and began attaching it to the Nikon. Crane got a glimpse of something else in the glove compartment, something that, although metallic, didn't look anything like a camera attachment.

"Have you got a gun in there?" he asked her.

She didn't look up from the Nikon she was fussing with. "I might have."

"You *might* have a gun in there."

"Okay, I have a gun in there. All right?"

"How'd it get there? Or did it just grow there, organically?"

"I put it there, what do you think?"

"Boone, that's it. That's the end." He started turning the key in the ignition.

She reached for his hand and stopped him. Gently.

"The gun used to be Patrick's. He left it with me."

"He took the furniture, and left the gun. What a guy."

"He didn't leave it on purpose. He forgot it. Look, I don't like the damn thing. I never liked it when Patrick kept it in the house."

"Which is why you keep it in the car."

"Crane, think. You wouldn't be here if you didn't

92

figure there was a good possibility Mary Beth was murdered."

He said nothing.

"And if that *is* what happened to Mary Beth," she continued, "and if those other 'suicide' victims were murdered, too, then looking into it, like we're doing, could be a little risky, right?"

He said nothing.

"So," she said, "we just might have to protect ourselves."

She took the gun — a .38 — out of the glove compartment.

"Give me that!" Crane said.

She did.

"This isn't loaded, is it?" he asked.

"Of course it's loaded."

He stuck it under the seat.

"You got a choice, next time," he said, his face feeling hot. "You can bring me along, or the gun. Not both."

"There's the truck again."

He turned and looked back at the loading area. The flatbed, its tarp tied over a full load, was wheeling out. No one, not even the hard hat that had been there before, was around; no one checked them out: the clearing booth was still empty.

Boone sat recording all this with the Nikon.

The truck turned right onto the blacktop, away from them.

"I better drive." Boone said.

"No," said Crane. "I can handle it."

He waited a few minutes and then pulled out of the Kemco lot, after the flatbed.

"One of its back lights is broken," Boone said, pointing.

Ahead, one of the taillights on the rig glowed white.

"That's a break," she said. "You can stay back and still not lose sight of him."

Crane sat forward, back straight, hands gripping the wheel, intensity squeezing the nervousness, the fear, right out of him. A couple times he felt himself creeping up too close on the truck—which was going a nice legal fifty-five—and Boone eased him back. There were a few other cars on the road, and occasionally he was able to put one of them between him and the truck, the tarp on the back of which was flapping loose a bit, giving them a glimpse now and then of the black drums of waste sitting bunched in the back like illegal immigrants.

"Don't sweat losing him," she said. "I think I know where he's headed."

And she did.

From the blacktop that wove through Garden State farmland, the truck went to a four-lane highway, where it was easy to stay way back and not lose track of the white light on the truck's tail.

"You know where he's headed now?" Crane asked Boone.

"Maybe," she said.

Soon the truck turned off onto a toll bridge.

They pulled off. Waited till the truck was across. Then followed.

Once over the bridge, Boone said, "Welcome to Pennsylvania, Crane."

They were still on a four-lane.

"I've lost him," Crane said, hitting the steering wheel with the heel of his hand.

"No," said Boone, pointing. "He's just turning off. Up to the right. See him?"

And there was the white light of the rig as it turned onto an off-ramp.

Crane followed suit.

94

After fifteen miles of sporadic two-way traffic on a primary road, the truck turned off onto a blacktop.

"Has he spotted us?" Crane asked.

"No."

"He could be leading us out into nowhere to deal with us, you know."

"I don't think so. You've stayed well back. He hasn't seen us."

"I'm going past it anyway."

He did, not turning off at the blacktop, glancing down it as they drove by to see if the truck had pulled over, to wait for them.

But it hadn't: the white eye was getting smaller as the truck lumbered down the blacktop.

Crane turned around on a side road and went back. Followed the truck down the blacktop.

Or tried to.

"This time I did lose him," he said. "I got over-cautious, damnit."

"Keep going."

"It's no use. I blew it. He's gone."

"What's that?"

"What?"

"There's a sign up there."

And there was: white letters on green, SANITARY LANDFILL, with an arrow to the right, and another blacktop.

Crane pulled in. Slowly. Just around the corner was a second sign, black letters on white: DEAD END.

He paused. "What do you think?"

"We've come this far," she said.

He drove down the narrow blacktop. The clear, moonlit night gave them a good view of the land on either side: at the right the land was flat, with bare, black clay, ground that had been turned over, like farmland prepared for planting; at the left another stretch of similar ground dropped off into a deep man-made gulley, the earth scarred by bulldozer tracks, the ground ripped at various seams, as if the aftermath of an earthquake.

"Cut your lights," Boone told him.

He did.

They came around a bend and the road ended and opened out into a gravelled area, just in front of a chain-wire fence with gates and two signs, a small one — ALL TRUCKS MUST BE COVERED — and a larger one — SANITARY LANDFILL, with a permit number listed underneath, operating hours (8 AM to 4 PM Monday thru Friday, 8 AM to Noon Saturday), and regulations (Public access during operating hours only; Scavenging not permitted; Unauthorized disposal punishable by $100 fine). Beyond the chain-wire fence were a couple of tin sheds, a large one at left for equipment storage, probably, a smaller one at right that was apparently the office. Several bulldozers stood unattended. At the left and right were high ridges of earth that blocked anything else along the horizon from view, from this vantage point at least. In the center was the drop-off of a landfill ditch.

The flatbed was already inside the chain-wire fence. The two guys from the truck — the bruiser in the thermal jacket and his partner, a tall skinny guy in denim work clothes and heavy gloves — got down out of the truck and were joined by a couple of guys in hard hats and work jackets. One of the hard hats began using a small forklift truck to unload the fifty-five-gallon barrels from the flatbed. The truckers helped him, guided the drums onto the forklift. The other hard hat watched and waited.

Boone used her Nikon.

It took over an hour to unload the truck and haul each drum over and dump it. Crane wondered why

96

he and Boone hadn't left yet; but she was still taking pictures, onto her second roll, now.

Then the hard hat who'd been standing, watching, climbed up on one of the bulldozers and started it up. It rumbled over to the landfill ditch. From where Crane and Boone were they couldn't see it, exactly, but it was clear what the bulldozer was doing: the drums were being covered with a layer of dirt.

"Those truckers won't be needing to hang around," Crane whispered. "We better take off before *they* do."

"Okay," Boone said, still snapping the Nikon.

Crane backed out, around the corner, turning the car around in the road in five long, slow turns, expecting the headlights of the flatbed to bear down on them momentarily.

But that didn't happen.

And they exited the blacktop onto the other blacktop and drove and, as they neared the four-lane that would lead them to the toll bridge and New Jersey, Boone said, "There's a motel over there. What do you think? I'm dead."

"I wouldn't mind stopping myself," he said.

They took a room. It had two double beds. Boone took a shower, came out in a towel and discreetly got into one of the beds. She then began snoring.

He smiled. He didn't blame her for being tired: it was four-thirty in the morning, and the intensity of what they'd just been through had been draining.

He didn't bother with a shower; he was too exhausted. He got in the other bed and was just about asleep when he heard a truck out on the highway. Just a truck going by.

He went out to the Datsun, got the gun out from under the seat, and slipped it under the bed.

Then he slept.

14

Her voice woke him.

She wasn't talking to him; she was on the phone, checking in with the neighbor she'd left Billy with, another young divorced woman who'd been very nice about looking after the boy from midnight till two each night, no questions asked. Boone had explained to her friend that any one of the nights might turn into an all-night thing, as it had yesterday.

"Billy got off to school all right?" she was saying. "Good. Thank you, Kate, you're a pal."

Boone was sitting on the edge of the bed Crane was in, using the phone on the nightstand between the two beds. Her back was to him. Bare back.

Soon she hung up and went over and got back in her own bed, sitting up, blankets down around her waist. She stretched and yawned. Scratched her head. Her hair was tousled. Her breasts were not large, not small. Firm white breasts, delicately veined; pert pink tips. He noted this through eyes that pretended to be shut.

She smiled at him. "You're awake, aren't you, Crane?"

He opened his eyes. Smiled sheepishly.

She didn't cover her breasts.

"Good morning," she said.

"Hi," he said. Sitting up.

She got out of bed and walked bare-ass into the bathroom. Water ran in the sink.

She came back out, smiling. Her body was very lean, with a high, rather bony rib cage, making her breasts seem larger than they were. Her pubic triangle was wispy, like a young girl's.

She sat on the edge of the bed, hands on her knees. "Go rinse out your mouth," she said. "You'll feel better. It's not like having toothbrush and paste, but it'll help."

He did so. He was in his shorts but still felt embarrassed walking in front of her, knowing she was looking him over just as he had her. When he came back, she was in bed. His bed.

He got in with her and kissed her, tentatively. She kissed him back, not at all tentatively, and put one of his hands on one of her breasts. The nipple hardened. He was already hard. They kissed and stroked each other for a while. Made love.

It was over rather quickly, too quickly, and he rolled off her, feeling empty.

"Sorry," he said.

"What are you apologizing about?" she said. "That was nice."

He sat up in bed and stared at the blank TV screen across the room.

A minute went by, and she said, leaning on an elbow, studying him, "You're going morose on me, aren't you?"

"What?"

"You're feeling guilty. You're thinking about Mary Beth and feeling guilty."

"Don't be silly."

"You think you cheated on her, don't you?"

"Boone, please."

She touched his shoulder. Not wanting to, he looked

at her. Her smile was faint, sad, understanding; it was a smile he couldn't evade.

He looked away and said, "Don't be with anybody else, she said. 'Don't be with anybody but me.' I can still hear her saying it."

"She's gone, Crane."

"No. Never."

He cried for a while; she kept her hand on his shoulder.

She said, "This was the first time I've done it since Patrick."

He looked at her again. "No kidding?"

She wiped his eyes with a corner of the sheet, smiling, her chin crinkling. "No kidding."

"I thought you hippie types slept around."

"Don't believe everything you hear. I was with two other boys, before Patrick. Nobody since. Until now."

"I've never been with anybody but Mary Beth. Till now."

"No wonder you're feeling guilty."

"I'm not feeling guilty. Exactly."

"I know you loved her, Crane. And me, you don't even like, exactly. But this was bound to happen, and I'd rather it happen here than at home where Billy might see us."

"Now who's sounding guilty?"

"I just want it clear that when we get back to the house, you're to keep to your sleeping bag across the hall."

"Fine. I like sleeping on the floor. It's natural. Organic, even."

"Smart-ass. I'm not saying it won't happen between us again. Billy's at school all day, you know."

He leaned over and kissed her, briefly. They exchanged friendly smiles.

100

"Looks like we're starting to get along," he said.

"Why not? We're quite the team. We're about to bring a corporate giant to its knees."

"Are we?"

"I think so. I think we really got something last night."

"The 'smoking gun' you said you needed."

"Exactly."

"So where do we go from here?"

"I admit I'm tempted to sit on this, save it and use it in my book, not break it till then. But the right thing to do is contact the proper authorities."

"Which are?"

"There's a couple of possibilities. New Jersey's a heavily industrialized state. It has more than its share of problems of this sort, but it's also ahead of a lot of states in dealing with those problems."

"So you'll be taking your photographs and your suspicions to a state agency, as opposed to the feds."

"The Environmental Protection Agency, you mean? They basically just provide guidelines to state agencies, though in a way they're who I'll be going to. I plan to go to the Hazardous Waste Strike Force, in Princeton."

"That sounds like a cop show."

"It is, sort of. It's an investigative unit, a joint effort by the EPA and the state of New Jersey. They're doing some good things."

"But they've never nailed Kemco."

"They never tried, as far as I know. And they're relatively new. Which means they're tackling the really blatant offenders. It's a big problem, Crane. It's been estimated something like 80% of the waste shipped in New Jersey is illegally dumped. It's a multimillion-dollar racket."

"What we saw last night was just one truck. That's no multimillion-dollar operation."

"First, you got to think of what Kemco saves. They pay maybe fifty bucks a barrel to the hauler, which is sure cheaper than processing that foul fucking shit. And then the hauler takes it and dumps it in a landfill, like last night, or just on the ground someplace or even along a roadside. So last night they dumped, what? Fifty or sixty drums? That's approaching $3000 for that one load. Let's say that truck is picking up just *one* illegal load per week. That's $150,000 in one year."

"Jesus. This is starting to sound like organized crime."

"Of course it is. It's the goddamn Mafia, or anyway I wouldn't be surprised if it was."

"What happens when these people get caught?"

"The haulers? Sometimes nothing. You want to know how to make a million dollars? Rent some land. Don't buy it, rent it. Get a permit to pick up and store drums of waste on your land. Let the drums pile up. Wait till you have twenty or thirty thousand drums sitting there, full of Christ knows what. And then go bankrupt and go away. Let the state worry about cleaning up after you. Just lean back in your cabana chair and sip your Piña Colada and enjoy the Bahamas breeze."

"Is that the game Chemical Disposal Works is playing?"

"Probably. They haven't gone bankrupt yet, but give 'em time."

"That's scary."

"You're goddamn right it's scary. But the way I figure it, you just write the haulers off. Forget about them. They're just lowlife fucking criminals, and there will *always* be lowlife fucking criminals around to do

102

the shitwork for the likes of Kemco. It's *Kemco* and the other corporations like it that have to be stopped. That have to be made to clean up their acts or else."

"Or else what?"

"Criminal penalties. Civil penalties. People are going to jail, Crane."

"That's it, then, isn't it?"

"What?"

"This is what Mary Beth and the others were onto. The midnight hauling. It *is* something that could've got them killed."

"Of course. Of course! What do you think I've been talking about for the last three days?"

"But what do you have on them, Boone, really? Just some photos. A truck coming out of the Kemco plant. A truck being unloaded at a landfill. Photos that could've been taken any time."

"No, Crane. We have pictures of a truck leaving Kemco at night, driving to an out-of-state landfill *at night*, where fifty or sixty drums were dumped. All very suspicious. And I have a feeling that the license plates on that truck will lead to some independent hauler with a less-than-spotless reputation. No, we have quite a lot for the Hazardous Waste boys to go on."

"It still strikes me as . . ."

"Let me guess. Thin? It strikes you as thin? Pearl Harbor would strike you as thin, Crane. Understand this much: New Jersey has a manifest system, and what that means is paperwork; every drum of hazardous waste that exits a plant like Kemco's is supposed to be recorded, from 'cradle to grave,' which is to say from Kemco, to the hauler, to the landfill. Do you suppose all the correct paperwork was filed for last night's moonlight dumping? Of course not."

"Jesus."

"Starting to dawn on you, is it Crane? Just what

103

it is we're into? Still want me to leave the gun at home?"

Crane managed an embarrassed smile as he reached under the bed, pulled the gun out and handed it to her. "Maybe you ought to start wearing this in your belt," he told her.

She returned his smile, put the gun on the night-stand, with a clunk. "There's nothing to worry about," she said. "Kemco doesn't know we're alive."

"They knew Mary Beth was alive. And now she isn't."

"Well at least you seem to be accepting it."

"What? That Mary Beth's dead? Or that 'Kemco killed her.' *People* killed her, Boone. Corporations don't kill people. People kill people."

"You sound like a bumper sticker."

"Fuck you," he said, good-naturedly.

"I thought you'd never ask," she said.

Fifteen minutes later, as they were dressing, Boone said, "I don't hear you apologizing, this time around."

"What's to apologize for? I was terrific."

"You weren't bad. Where's the camera?"

"Why? What did you have in mind?"

"No, seriously."

"Didn't you bring it in with you?"

"I was so tired last night all I could think about was flopping into bed. I must've left it in the car. Anyway, I want to get that film developed this afternoon. Do you want to come to Princeton with me?"

"No. I still have some people in Greenwood to talk to. I think you can handle the 'Hazardous Waste Strike Force' by yourself . . . though the notion of seeing you trying to work with some Jack Webb type tempts me to go along."

"You can stay home and baby-sit with Billy."

"Ouch."

They were ready to leave.

Crane opened the door for her. "There's a coffee shop down by the motel office. You want some breakfast?"

"Sure. Walk down or drive?"

"Drive. Why not be lazy?"

They got in the car.

The camera was gone.

"Shit!" Boone said.

They had searched the car thoroughly, looked all around it, underneath it, checked with the motel manager, everything. The camera was gone. Now they stood next to the car, one on either side of it, its doors standing open. Stood and stared at the car as if it might speak to them. It didn't.

"Shit, shit, shit," she said.

"Boone," Crane said.

"Cocksuckers. The cocksuckers!"

A man a few doors down from their room was coming out of his; he looked at them with wide eyes, having heard what Boone just said, then walked quickly past them toward the coffee shop, looking at the ground as he did.

"Boone," Crane said. "Please settle down."

"Settle down my ass!"

He closed the car doors.

She was pacing. Then she stopped and pointed a finger at him.

"Now what do you think, skeptic? *Now* what do you think?"

"I think we ought to have some breakfast."

"You think we ought to have some breakfast. You're unbelievable."

"Let's have some breakfast and talk about this before we head back."

She paced some more.

Then she said, "Okay. All right."

She walked ahead of him. She walked fast, propelled by anger. He followed her into the small coffee shop and they took a booth by a window overlooking the highway. Trucks were rolling by, normally an innocuous enought sight; not today.

He ordered coffee and some biscuits; she asked for tea, in a tone of voice that scared the waitress.

"Take it easy, Boone."

"Jesus you're a wimp."

"Boone. Just settle down."

"Aren't you mad, Crane? Aren't you the slightest bit pissed off?"

"Of course I am. It's just at the moment, you seem to have the hysteria market cornered."

She let go a wry little smile at that; couldn't help herself.

"You've made your point," she conceded. "But do you realize what this means?"

"What does it mean."

"Somebody knows what we're up to. It means somebody's trying to stop us."

He took one of her hands in two of his. He smiled at her in such a way as to remind her, he hoped, that they'd been in bed together not too long ago.

"Boone," he said, "I admit it's possible we were seen by those truckers last night. That they followed us and stole the camera."

She pulled her hand away. "Possible? What else could 'it have been?"

"Maybe your ex is on to your Kemco investigation. Maybe we were seen in your Datsun staking out the place."

She thought about that.

"You think it might have been somebody from Patrick's end of it who took the camera? Not the truckers."

"Possibly," he shrugged. "We were following the truck. Maybe somebody was following us."

She thought about that, too.

The coffee and biscuits came; the tea, too.

"And," Crane said, quietly, carefully, "there's another possibility."

"Which is?"

"Somebody walked by and saw a camera in the car and stole it."

"What?"

"Back in Iowa, when you leave a camera in an unlocked car overnight, you aren't shocked when it's gone the next morning. Is it different in New Jersey?"

"Pennsylvania."

"Well, that makes all the difference."

"Somebody happened along and just stole it, you mean. Just coincidentally stole it."

"Boone, there's nothing coincidental about a hundred-and-fifty-buck camera getting stolen out of an unlocked car."

She slammed a small but china-rattling fist against the tabletop betweem them. People were looking at them.

"You just won't believe it, will you, Crane? You just aren't capable of accepting what's *really* happening here."

He sipped his coffee. Waited for some of the eyes to stop staring. Then he smiled at her. Calmly. "It's not that. I'm frightened, if that's what you want to hear. I personally agree with you that somebody, those truckers or your ex-husband or *somebody* related to Mary Beth's 'suicide,' took that camera out of your

108

Datsun while we slept a few feet away, and it further frightens me, it frightens fuck out of me in fact, to think that we might never've stopped sleeping, if whoever it was had come those few feet closer."

"I'm glad you're finally looking at this rationally."

"Rationally? I'm telling you my emotional reaction, Boone. Gut feelings. My mind tells me, rationally tells me, that the camera was probably stolen by some doper looking for something to hock."

"Shit!" she said.

People were looking at them again. Crane glared at them and they stopped looking.

She was leaning against the tabletop, her hands on her forehead.

"You know I'm right, don't you?" he said.

"You're not right. Somebody wanted that film destroyed. That's why the camera was stolen."

"Maybe. I'll go as far as probably. But we can't prove it. That's the point I'm trying to make. We have *nothing*, Boone. Not a goddamn thing."

They sat in silence for a while. He finished his coffee and biscuits. She drank two cups of tea. Then without a word she rose, picking up the check and paying for it, and walked out to her car. He followed her. She acted as if he weren't there.

They were well into New Jersey before she acknowledged his presence again.

"I'm still going to Princeton this afternoon," she said, driving.

"I don't know that it'll do any good."

"I want to tell the Strike Force what happened. What we saw. That we took pictures and our camera was stolen."

"Okay."

"It might be enough to make them go out and check the landfill. See what sort of shit is in those drums."

109

"Boone, if the truckers did see us leaving the site, and followed us, don't you think they'd have gone back and dug the drums up and hauled them away?"

"Maybe. But I have to try, Crane. Do you understand that?"

"Of course. I'm on your side, you know."

She smiled over at him. Reached over and touched his face. "I know. I don't mean to treat you like the enemy."

"Assuming there *is* an enemy," Crane said.

"Are you starting up again?"

"No. I'm not going to Princeton with you, though."

"I know. You're going to look after Billy for me, and talk to a few people."

"Right."

"I should be back by midnight."

"Good. Uh, Boone."

"Yes?"

"Nothing."

He took the gun out of his jacket pocket and put it back in her glove compartment.

Mrs. Paul Meyer lived in a pale yellow house in the same housing development as Mary Beth's family. Just a block down, in fact. The major difference between the two houses, other than color, was the For Sale sign in the Meyer lawn.

Mrs. Meyer had told Crane on the phone that he was free to drop by any time after lunch and before her children got home from school. It was now two in the afternoon.

He knocked on the door.

She opened the door slowly and looked at Crane the same way. She was slender, about thirty, with short dark hair and piercing, pretty eyes as dark as her hair; her lips were a thin red line as she appraised him, tilting her head back a bit so she could look down on him, a hand poised at the base of her neck, around which hung a thin gold chain, which settled comfortably in the soft folds of silk of her cream-colored blouse.

The glass of the storm door still separating them, she said, "Yes?" and he told her who he was and she gave him a small twitch of a smile and let him in.

This split-level house was built from the same plans as Mary Beth's family's home, and it was disturbing to be in a living room so much like the one he sat in with Mary Beth's mother a few days ago. Even the furniture was similarly arranged—the couch was opposite the front door as you came in—but on a closer look it began to look quite different. The furniture, here, was antique: walnut, mostly. Expensive. Tasteful.

Like Mrs. Meyer, who stood in front of him with a glacially polite smile, one hand on a trim hip (she wore rather clingy black slacks), the other gesturing toward the brocade couch.

He sat. So did she. Across from him, in a love seat.

"I'm sorry about your fiancée, Mr. Crane," she said.

You couldn't tell it by her voice.

"Thank you," he said. "I appreciate your willingness to see me."

"I don't understand why you want to talk to me, actually. I do understand that we have something in common." She got up and walked to the coffee table between them, where she took a cigarette from a silver box and lit it. Pulled smoke into her lungs, let it out, sat down again. "My Paul killed himself. Your Mary Beth killed herself. Tragic. But not uncommon."

Not in Greenwood, anyway, he thought.

"Could I ask you a few questions, Mrs. Meyer?"

"If you like."

"When did your husband die?"

"Six months ago. He shot himself in the temple." She smiled. "That's a punch line you know."

"Pardon me?"

"Punch line of an old 'sick' joke. One man says to the other man, did you hear about Jones? The other man says, no I didn't. The first man says, killed himself. The second man says, no!, how did it happen? The first man says, shot himself in the temple. And the second man says, that's funny—he didn't look Jewish." She smiled again. A forced smile. Her eyes were a little wet.

112

"I shouldn't be intruding. I can go . . ."

"You can go if you like. That little story is as close to coming unglued as I'm going to get. So you don't have to worry, Mr. Crane."

"Mrs. Meyer, you and I have more in common than just having someone we loved commit suicide."

"You presume quite a bit."

"Pardon?"

"You presume I loved Paul."

"Didn't you?"

"Yes. But what does that have to do with you?"

"I better go."

"If you like. I don't mean to be rude. Really. I've invited you into my home. I've agreed to talk with you. It's just that I want to make clear that I'm not a person to turn to in your hour of grief. I have no free advice for you on how to handle this situation. Just because I happen to be somebody else whose . . . loved one died of self-inflicted wounds, doesn't mean . . ." She stopped herself. Her eyes were getting wet again. She waved some smoke from her cigarette away from her face.

"Mrs. Meyer. I'm not here for that. I'm not here for . . . group therapy, or something."

She looked surprised for a moment. "Why *are* you here, then?"

"As I started to say, we have more in common than just the suicides of Mary Beth and your husband. Or rather I should say that *they* had more in common than suicide."

"What do you mean?" The words were clipped.

"They both worked at Kemco."

"So?"

"Are you aware that there have been five suicides in Greenwood, in not much more than a year? And that all five victims worked for Kemco?"

113

"A lot of people around here work for Kemco."

"Five suicides, Mrs. Meyer. Ten times the national average."

She thought about that a moment. "That's an interesting random statistic. But I don't see your point."

"It just seems suspicious to me, is all. My fiancée was not the type of person who would commit suicide. I doubt she did commit suicide. I think it was something else."

"Such as what?"

"Something else."

She got up, put her cigarette out in an ashtray on the coffee table. She sat back down. She and the empty side of the love seat stared at him. "What do you want from me?" she asked.

"I want to ask you a few questions."

"Ask, then."

"Did your husband know Mary Beth?"

"I really don't know."

"He never mentioned her? She was working out of the secretarial pool."

"I never heard him mention her. I never heard of her at all, until a friend told me a young woman down the street killed herself. Where is this heading?"

"Do you have any suspicions about your husband's suicide? If you don't mind my asking."

"No, I haven't any suspicions, and yes I mind."

"Mrs. Meyer, I have reason to believe Kemco is and has been involved in some illegal practices. I think it's possible that Mary Beth and possibly your husband and others among those 'suicides' may have been well aware of those practices, and . . . well, now you should be able to see where I'm headed."

She stood. "There," she said. She was pointing at the front door. "That's where you're headed."

He got up. "I'll be glad to leave. I know I'm intruding. Please excuse me and I'll go."

"You'll go, but not till I've had my say. My husband killed himself. There's no doubt in my mind that he did. He had emotional problems, which I'd rather not discuss with a stranger. They were problems that ran deep. He had them before he met me. We tried to work them out together. We failed, or I failed, or maybe he failed. But one night he went in his study, where he sometimes slept, and in the morning I found him dead. By his own hand. By his own hand, Mr. Crane!"

"Please, Mrs. Meyer . . ."

"Kemco was one of the few things in Paul's life that he was satisfied with. He was assistant plant manager, and he had a good future . . . this was just a first, small step for him with the company. I'll tell you something about Kemco, Mr. Crane. Paul lied to them when he filled out his application forms; he withheld information, namely that he had been in a mental institution, and more than once. This came out, after Paul's suicide, of course. But they are paying me the full pension due Paul. Which they have no legal obligation to do."

"Doesn't that seem suspicious to you?"

"Suspicious?" She raised a tiny fist as if to strike him, then quickly lowered it. "It seems humane. It seems very moral. It does *not* seem suspicious. Don't badmouth Kemco around me, Mr. Crane. The Kemco people have been kind to me. Generous. I think your suspicions, your accusations, are as irresponsible as they are unfounded."

"I do have suspicions. But I'm not making any accusations."

"By implication you are. Mr. Crane. I don't mean

to fly off the handle at you. I'm not a cold person, really. I, if anyone, can understand how you feel. What you're going through. You can say you didn't come here for advice, and I said I wouldn't give you any if you asked. But I do have some. Let go of her. Your fiancée. Let her die. Let her be dead. Accept it. Go on living. Stop this vain attempt to place the blame for what happened on somebody or some thing. Even if someone *was* to blame, she'd still be dead."

He couldn't tell her, didn't know how to tell her, that this had gone beyond that; that he had started to share Boone's conviction that there was a criminal conspiracy, here, endangering lives.

So he just said, "Thank you. I'll think about what you've said."

"Good," she said, smiling her thin red line, extending her hand, which he took and shook, as a way of signing a truce.

And he left her, standing in the doorway, watching him go.

Even a block away, as he walked by Mary Beth's, he could feel those dark eyes on his back.

The grade school was a one-story modern building on the west edge of town. It was approaching three o'clock. Crane stood near the playground across from the school, leaning against a telephone pole, watching school buses pull up for the farm kids, while older kids, who served as crossing guards, were getting in place at the curb.

He didn't imagine too many of the kids would be making a beeline for this playground, which was a dreary little place, just a flat piece of land running back to a fence that separated it from the backyards of some modest, modern homes. There was a jungle gym, slide, swings and so on on it, but no trees or bushes, just some puddles scattered around, from a recent rain.

Soon the kids were streaming out from the school, and among them was Boone's kid, Billy. He was wearing a blue zipper jacket and striped T-shirt and jeans. And a sullen expression. Or at least the expression was sullen once he'd seen Crane.

"What do *you* want?" he said.

"Your mom isn't home right now," Crane told the boy.

"So?"

"I just thought you should know."

"I can walk home by myself. You aren't walking me."

"I'm not here for that, Billy. I came to talk to some-

117

body at the school. But I wanted to catch you so you didn't wonder why the house was empty when you got home."

"Well. Okay."

"I'll be home in a little while."

"I don't care."

The boy walked away. Another little boy, a tow-headed kid in a denim jacket, joined Billy. They roughhoused as they walked along, picked up some rocks from the playground and hurled them at each other, narrowly missing, the rocks careening off the sidewalk, flashing bright colors. Crane supposed he ought to tell Billy to quit throwing rocks, but as much as he liked Boone, he just couldn't find it in him to give a damn about her bratty kid.

He entered the school and went to the front office and was directed to room 714, where Mrs. Alma Price was waiting for him.

She was behind her desk, grading some papers. Behind her, on the blackboard (which was green), were some multiplication problems and a geography assignment. The little tan-topped desks that filled the fourth-grade classroom seemed very small to Crane, incredibly small compared to the fourth-grade classroom in his memory.

Alma Price was a redheaded woman in her late forties, not unpleasantly plump, with a wide attractive face and the same sort of smile, which she gave Crane generously as she rose from behind her desk, smoothing out her green dress, greeting him with an outstretched hand.

He shook it and smiled back.

"There's a normal-size chair over there," she said, gesturing to one corner, as she returned to her desk. "Pull it up and we'll talk."

He did so.

118

"I hope you don't mind my asking to see you here at school," she said, still smiling, but some strain in the smile, now.

"Not at all," he said. "I'm just grateful you were willing to put up with this."

"Having gone through something very similar to what you are, I'm more than happy to give you whatever benefit my experience might give you. I take it Mary Beth must've mentioned me."

That caught him by surprise.

"Uh, no," he said.

That caught her by surprise.

"Why did you come to see me then? Who told you that Mary Beth had been a student of mine?"

"No one," Crane admitted. "I didn't know. I'm fascinated to find it out, but I didn't know."

She pushed her hands against the edge of her desk, as if about to rise, but remained seated, studying Crane. "Then just what are you doing here, Mr. Crane?"

"As I said on the phone, I'm aware that you lost your husband, several months ago . . ."

"Seven months ago."

"And that like Mary Beth, he committed suicide."

"In our garage. Shut himself in there, stuffed all the air openings with cloth, turned on the car and lay down near the tail pipe. He went to sleep and never woke up."

She said that matter-of-factly, but there was a tremble under it.

"I'm sorry, Mrs. Price."

"I'm sorry about Mary Beth. I'm sorry for you. She'd have been a wonderful wife. Now. Excuse me, please, Mr. Crane, but what exactly brought you to me? Is it simply the fact that we both have suffered the suicides of someone we loved? If so, I will try to help.

But I'll be frank: time won't heal the wound. You'll learn to live with it, but you won't forget it, and it won't heal over. I'm sorry, but that, I'm afraid, is the reality of it."

"Mrs. Price, your advice is appreciated, and taken to heart, believe me. But it's not why I'm here. I'm here because there is something your husband and Mary Beth had in common beyond suicide."

She nodded. "They both worked for Kemco."

"You knew that?"

"Of all the students I ever had, Mary Beth was my favorite. Of all the teachers she ever had, I was her favorite. I kept track of her. She kept in touch with me. Of course I knew she was in town this summer, working for Kemco. Of course I knew that."

"I think Mary Beth may not have committed suicide, Mrs. Price. I think it may have only looked like suicide. I think it may have had something to do with Kemco."

"I see."

"You don't sound surprised."

"I don't know what I am. But 'surprised' isn't it."

"Then you had similar suspicions about your husband's death?"

"Yes. Of course."

"And?"

"I eventually dismissed them."

"Why?"

"It's natural to want to explain away the suicide of your husband. Or wife, or fiancée. It's human to want to reject the notion that someone you loved, someone that loved you, would want to end his or her life."

"So you decided your suspicions were groundless?"

"Not groundless. But I did decide that they were just suspicions and nothing more."

"Why do I sense there's something you're not telling me?"

"There's much I'm not telling you."

"Mrs. Price, this is very important to me. I think you can understand how important."

"Of course I can. But I don't want to encourage this . . . excuse me, obsession of yours."

"Do I sound obsessed?"

"No. You seem rational. In control. But that's your outward appearance. I believe that, inside, you're avoiding reality. That you will do whatever you have to to convince yourself Mary Beth did not take her life."

"Was your husband the sort of man who would take his life?"

"Yes. He did, after all."

"And you're convinced of that."

"I am. I can see there's no way around this. I'm going to have to share something personal with you. I'd like not to. But I will if you insist. And I'm going to make you insist, Mr. Crane."

"Please, Mrs. Price."

"If you insist. My husband, George, had a problem. The problem was my first husband. My late first husband, by whom I had two children, boy in college, daughter married and here in town with children of her own. I married just out of high school, and it wasn't until my first husband died, fifteen years ago, that I went to college. You see my first husband's name also was George. George Waters. I loved him very much. He died of cancer, when he was just thirty-seven years old. You know he seemed so much older than me when we were married; I always thought of him as being so old. And now I'm forty-seven, ten years older than he was when he died. Well. So three years ago my other George came along. A sweet, caring man. When we were just seeing each other, we had no problems. After we married, well . . . the coincidence of having the same name as my first husband started to bother him. He didn't like it when my friends would talk about my late husband, referring to him as 'the first George,' or 'George the First.' He came to resent my two children, both of whom were grown by the time he came into my life. He was jealous of a memory, which to make it worse had his same name. He seldom would discuss his frustrations about my late husband; he just brooded about it. Sometimes he drank. For the year before he took his life, he was quite depressed."

"All because he and your first husband shared the same first name?"

"And the same wife, don't forget. And similar jobs."

"Oh?"

"Both of them worked in maintenance at Kemco. My first husband didn't have as good a job as my second, who was head of the maintenance crew. But it was in the same area. And the coincidence of it bothered him."

"I admit it's kind of strange, but why get obsessed with it?"

"George—the second George—worked at another chemical processing plant in the Midwest, before coming to Greenwood. It wasn't a Kemco facility; I believe it was Monsanto. He felt Kemco was . . . this is what I hesitate to get into with you because I'm afraid it will only serve to reinforce *your* obsession."

"Mrs. Price. Please go on."

"He felt Kemco was borderline negligent. At the other plant he worked at, when the government would hand down a pollution level, for example, the company would set its own, stricter policy, well below what

122

the government would allow. But at Kemco, George said, they would push it to the limit, and beyond, if they felt they could get away with it."

"I see."

"And he generally felt that the safety procedures at the local plant were lax. He and other workers had been exposed to dangerous chemicals, hazardous substances. But he could never do anything about it. Neither management nor union seemed to care. He said."

"I'm still not sure if I understand how this relates to his obsession about your first husband."

"Simple. He thought he was getting cancer."

"Was he?"

"I have no way of knowing. He would never see a doctor about it."

"Was there an autopsy?"

"Yes, and nothing was turned up."

"But cancer wasn't what they were looking for."

"If it was advanced, they'd have found it."

"If it was in beginning stages, they might not."

"Possibly. But it was probably all just the delusion of a jealous, neurotic man. The 'other' George caught cancer working at Kemco, so now the same thing was happening to him. He thought."

"Do you think there could be any truth to it?"

"I don't know."

"Do you know a friend of Mary Beth's named Anne Boone?"

"Yes, I've met her. She's doing research of some sort, gathering data on Greenwood itself. She interviewed me, several months ago."

"But you didn't tell her all of what you've told me."

"No. Judging from the questions she asked, she would've been interested in hearing about my husband's concerns about safety and other problems at Kemco. But I didn't tell her."

"Why are you telling me?"

"I don't really know. How do you happen to know about my conversation with Ms. Boone?"

"I've heard the tape of it."

She stiffened. "Oh really?"

"It's all right — I'm working with Ms. Boone. We're compiling evidence that may show Kemco negligent in several areas . . . including the areas that concerned your husband. Are you aware that the cancer rate in Greenwood is well above the national average?"

"No . . ."

"And the same is true for birth defects, and miscarriages. Not to mention the suicide rate: five suicides in not much more than a year. All by Kemco employees."

"I take it you don't believe they're suicides."

"Not all of them. At least one does seem to be a legitimate suicide."

"Of course. The man who shot himself and his family. I remember. I had the children in school."

"But I suspect Mary Beth had information about Kemco's negligence, which may have cost her her life."

"And you think my husband had the same or similar information?"

"If he was as obsessed with Kemco's negligence as you say he was, wouldn't he have sought it out?"

She thought about that.

Then she rose.

"Mr. Crane," she said, and from her tone it was clear school was being dismissed, "I have work to do."

Crane got out of the chair, put it back where he'd found it.

He said, "I hope you'll think about what I've said."

"I will. But I have to warn you. I don't share my late husband's opinions where Kemco is concerned. Kemco has a solid record of civic concern in Greenwood. They donated the land this school is built on. They provide work for many of our city's residents. Some of the people who run that plant are former students of mine. I'm seeing a man right now who is employed there. So don't look at me as an ally. I'm still of the opinion that you are very much on the wrong track. George killed himself. As much as I hate to think it, I'm afraid Mary Beth did the same."

"I'm staying at Ms. Boone's, if you think of anything else I should know."

"I doubt you'll be hearing from me."

"Well, just in case."

"All right. Now, I don't like to seem ungracious, but I do have papers to mark."

He said, "Of course," and walked to the door.

As he was about to go out, he heard her voice from behind him: "If we do talk again, Mr. Crane, perhaps I could tell you about Mary Beth. Some things I remember about her from when she was in my class."

"Was it this classroom?" Crane asked.

"Yes. The first year the school was built. First class I ever taught."

"Where did she sit?"

"That seat to your left. Last one in the third row."

Crane walked over to it and touched the back of the seat.

Then he went to the door, turned and said, "We'll talk again," and left.

He walked the several blocks to Boone's house, confused, not knowing quite what to make of Mrs. Price. Or Mrs. Meyer, for that matter. He was almost on top of it before he noticed the blue Chrysler with the Kemco logo on the door, parked in front of Boone's house.

A guy in his twenties with short black hair, mustache and a short-sleeved white shirt with black-and-

125

white striped tie got out of the car and said, "Are you Crane?"

"Yes."

"Boone would like to talk with you."

Boone? What would she have to do with this guy? Then he understood.

"Patrick Boone, you mean?"

"That's right," the guy said. "He said if you're willing to come talk, I'm to give you a lift out to Kemco."

Crane got in the car.

This was the first time he'd seen the Kemco plant in the daytime, and it seemed less impressive, and not at all sinister: the sheets of mottled aqua plastic that were the walls of the larger buildings looked somehow insubstantial, houses of cards that might topple momentarily; the pipes twining in and out and around these plastic-sheeted structures reminded him of the jungle gym in that dreary little playground he'd been standing near just an hour or so before.

The drive here had taken fifteen minutes but it had been a long ride just the same: the guy with the short black hair and mustache and black-and-white striped tie did not introduce himself and did not speak for the ride's duration; he did push a tape into the player in the dash of the company car: Willie Nelson. Crane had hoped people in the East didn't listen to Willie Nelson; no such luck.

He felt a nervousness in his stomach, like opening-night butterflies. But he wasn't scared. He knew that if Mary Beth had been murdered, Patrick Boone was very likely, in some way, shape or form, involved. But he didn't fear for his life, not sitting in a Chrysler with a Willie Nelson fan in a tie; not pulling up in front of a chemical plant that in the daylight looked anything but ominous.

Anxious was what he felt. He wondered why Boone's ex-husband had called him out here. Was the man really onto what he and Boone had been doing? Would he toss Boone's empty Nikon in Crane's lap? Or maybe one of the people he'd been asking questions of called up Patrick Boone and informed him somebody named Crane was nosing around; Mrs. Meyer, the Kemco loyalist, most likely.

The executive offices of the plant were in a sprawling one-story building just off the parking lot, near the ever-flapping American flag. The nameless junior exec led him through a surprisingly shabby, claustrophobic lobby where a pair of plaid-upholstered couches met at a corner of the room and shared an end table littered with chemical company trade magazines. Over one of the couches was a framed quote from the founder of Kemco (Willis P. Connor, 1880–1955): "Industry is people." A receptionist was walled within at right and the nameless exec spoke to her through a window, checking them in. The receptionist asked if they would need hard hats and safety glasses; the exec said no. Crane was glad. He followed the exec through a turnstile into a hallway.

The building was nothing fancy: tiled floors, plaster walls, tiled ceilings, as impersonal as this exec he was trailing after. There was a studied informality about the place: the people they passed in the halls all spoke, on a first name basis (the nameless exec's name was Chuck, it seemed) and wore white shirts and ties but with the coat invariably off, either over one arm or left behind. Doors on either side of the wide hall stood occasionally open, one of them revealing a laboratory wherein a dozen or so technicians worked. Another open door revealed several people attending computer terminals; another contained half a dozen desks with women of various ages typing—

had one of these desks been Mary Beth's? Then came closed doors, reading BOOKKEEPING DEPARTMENT, PRODUCTION SUPERINTENDENT, MAINTENANCE SUPERINTENDENT, PLANT MANAGER. They stopped at the door reading PERSONNEL MANAGER. Chuck opened the door for him, peeked in and said, "Mr. Crane to see Patrick, Sharen," turned to Crane and said, "Nice meeting you," and left. Crane stepped inside.

A pretty blonde secretary, in her own, small outer office, rose from her desk, smiled, and opened the door to the inner office for him, without announcing him. He went in.

Patrick Boone was already up and out from behind his desk with a hand extended for Crane to shake. He was a slender man, about Crane's size, pale, handsome, vaguely preppie, despite his hippie roots, with dark curly hair and, with the exception of a wispy mustache and wire frame glasses, the spitting image of his son Billy.

"I'm glad you agreed to come, Crane," Patrick Boone said as he shook Crane's hand, a firm, friendly shake. He smiled as he spoke. It wasn't a bad smile.

He got Crane a chair before getting behind the desk, where once seated, he said, "Can I order you up some coffee? Or something?"

Crane shrugged. "I could use a soft drink. Anything."

Patrick Boone smiled again, and Crane admitted to himself that if he were meeting the man cold, he'd probably like him. "Sharen," he was saying into his intercom, "a couple of Pepsies for us, if you would."

While they waited for the Pepsies, the preppie smile disappeared and he leaned forward, both arms on his desk.

"I can't tell you how sorry I am about Mary Beth," he said. "I only knew her slightly. She did a little work

129

for me. But my impression was she was a fine person."

"I didn't catch you at the funeral."

"I wasn't there. I didn't know her well enough to intrude on her family and friends. And, too, Annie would've been there."

"Annie?"

"My ex-wife. Let's not pretend you don't know her. I'd like us to be more up front than that."

The secretary, Sharen, brought the Pepsies in.

As she handed them around, she said, "I need to pick my son up after Scouts today. Do you mind if I leave a little early, Patrick?"

He glanced at his watch. "It's four-fifteen now. Why don't you just take off."

She beamed at him. "Thanks."

After she'd left, Patrick explained, "We don't stand on ceremony around here. We like to keep it a bit, uh . . ."

"Informal?"

"Yes."

"Mr. Boone . . ."

"Patrick."

"Patrick, then. I know your ex-wife. I won't pretend I don't. I just didn't know anybody called her 'Annie.' "

"Well, she's taken to being called just 'Boone,' these days. Some kind of feminist stand, I suppose. But if that's the case, why not revert to her maiden name?"

"Probably because she's raising your son."

"You're probably right. Well. I suppose you know why I asked you to stop by."

"Not really."

"I know what Annie's up to. Oh, maybe not exactly, I don't. But I know it's another one of her articles. Or maybe it's a series of articles."

He paused, perhaps hoping for Crane to enlighten him.

When Crane didn't, Patrick went on: "She's been asking questions around Greenwood for months. Researching Kemco. Trying to catch us doing something she doesn't approve of. Which won't be hard, considering anything any chemical company does would be something she wouldn't approve of."

"Maybe."

"Then you won't deny she's rather narrow-minded on the subject?"

"Well . . ."

"Surely the basis of her hatred of Kemco is apparent to you."

Crane said nothing.

"It's *me*, Crane. It's me she hates. Kemco's a surrogate. Or scapegoat or whatever you want to call it. A perfect target for her outdated late '60s/early '70s radical liberalism."

"Didn't you used to lean that way yourself?"

"Of course. Didn't you?"

"No."

"Well, then, but you're younger, aren't you, so that explains it. Almost everybody on college campuses in those days felt that way. You would've had to lived through the draft to understand. It was a valid enough point of view in its day, naive as it may have been. Some of us, like Annie, stay stuck in time. Some of us move on."

"Move on and sell out?"

He grinned, swigged the can of Pepsi, pushed back in his swivel chair. "For somebody who sold out, I lead a pretty drab existence, wouldn't you say?" he said, gesturing around an office that was four panelled walls and a couple of framed photos, one of the plant, the

131

other of the home office in St. Louis. "All I make is a little over thirty grand a year, a goodly chunk of which goes to Ms. Woman's Lib of 1969."

"You're young. You're moving up in the company."

"I will be. What's wrong with that? Don't you believe in capitalism, Crane?"

"The problem is I do. I do believe in it, and it pisses me off when I see it get twisted up."

"Boy, you *have* been listening to Annie, haven't you? She can be persuasive, I know. What kind of horror stories has she been telling you?"

"About you, or about Kemco?"

"Crane. Please. I want you to know something. I want you to know that I understand where you're coming from. Or at least I think I do. Hope I do. Shouldn't presume that I do, really. But I'm guessing that you took Mary Beth's suicide hard. That you found it hard to believe anyone as full of life as Mary Beth could end that life, voluntarily." He stopped and rubbed his forehead. "I'm sorry. I don't mean to sound so trite. To sound like I'm trivializing this. Christ. May I go on?"

"Yes."

"I think you ran into Annie. Possibly at the funeral, or maybe later at Mary Beth's mother's home, or whatever. And Annie filled your head with her crazy leftist lunacy. Normally you might not have bought it. But it was easier accepting what Annie was saying than accepting Mary Beth's death as suicide. I'm not far wrong, am I?"

Crane said nothing.

"I know that you've been asking some questions," Patrick said. "I know that you have some suspicions."

He'd been right: it *was* Mrs. Meyer. Patrick did not know about the trip to Pennsylvania last night. Did he?

"There *are* some disturbing statistics," Patrick was

132

saying. "We're aware of the number of suicides in Greenwood; we're aware of some illnesses that may be related to Kemco employees and their families. We'll be looking into it ourselves."

"I'll look forward to *that* investigation."

Patrick smiled sadly and shook his head. "She's really poisoned you, hasn't she? Don't you see it? Don't you see that this is a family squabble? That Annie is getting at me through the company I work for? I sold out, remember? It's not enough to attack me. She has to attack the institutions I sold out to."

"All because the poor kid's stuck in time."

"That's right. It's the '80s now, Crane, in case you haven't noticed. Damn near the '90s, chilling thought though that is."

"I noticed."

"How close to her are you?"

"What do you mean?"

"I understand you're staying at her house."

"I'm just crashing there."

"Crashing. There's a Woodstock-era word for you. Did she tell you why we split up?"

"No."

"Drugs."

"What do you mean?"

"I was doing drugs. Nothing much. Some hash. Some coke." His frankness was surprising, if somehow smug.

"You buy coke on thirty grand a year?"

He shrugged. "I dealt a little on the side. That upset her, too. Almost as much as me wearing a suit to work."

"She said she wasn't into drugs."

"She's lying. Oh, she isn't *now*. But back in our college days, she was deep in it, deeper than me. She dropped acid like you take Alka Seltzer."

"I don't take Alka Seltzer."

"Well you get my point. Then she reformed. There's nothing worse than a reformed *anything*. She got on her health-food kick. She read books and articles on the bad effects of acid. Same with pot, for Christsake. Said it ruined brain tissue, affected the sexual organs, some bullshit. I don't know. But she turned fanatic. I tried to do right by her. I stopped dealing. It was dangerous for me, anyway, now that I was with the company. I needed a straighter life-style. So no more coke, no more anything except smoke a little dope now and then. But even *that* was too much for her. I remember saying to her, the last generation liked its martinis, right? Well I like my pot. But that didn't cut it with her, because alcohol's on her shit list, too. It was like living with a religious fanatic. The screaming fucking arguments we had. Christ. But that's neither here nor there. It got to be too much."

"It broke up your marriage."

"Yeah. She was on a real guilt trip, and believe me, it all ties in with what she's doing now, where Kemco is concerned. She's worried she fucked up her chromosomes dropping acid. She's worried about Billy. The repercussions her doper days will have on our son."

"Aren't you worried?"

"No. I don't believe that alarmist bullshit. But she does."

"I'll tell you something. Maybe Boone's motivation for all this does stem from her hating you. But I've been reading up on some of your precious chemical industry, and some of what I read scares me."

He shrugged, swigged the last of the Pepsi. "Haven't you heard that TV commercial? Without chemicals, life itself would be impossible?"

"So would cancer."

"You really believe that bullshit Annie tells you?"

"I believe 350,000 Americans will die from cancer this year. And I believe the reason is largely chemical companies unleashing untried, untested chemical compounds on an unsuspecting environment."

"You even sound like her. Like a goddamn pamphlet. You're a writer yourself, I understand."

"I'm working on it."

"Studying journalism?"

"That's right."

"Everybody needs a hobby."

"Like dumping hazardous wastes in the middle of the night?"

Patrick sat up. "Some of that goes on. Not here."

"Are you sure?"

He shrugged. "I won't say some of it hasn't. I don't know that any's going on now. We have a manifest system in this state. We keep track of everything we dump."

"So you say."

"So we say. And if somebody says otherwise, they better be prepared to prove it."

"Maybe somebody will."

Patrick smiled. "It won't be you and Annie."

"Is that a threat?"

"No." He laughed. "Are you kidding? Annie has no credibility as a journalist. She's published a few pieces in minor league leftist nothings. You? You're just a grad student. She's the ex-wife of an exec at Kemco she wants to crucify. You have your own grudge, where your late fiancée is concerned. With credibility like that, you and Annie are finished before you start. Get serious."

"You're as much as admitting . . ."

"Nothing. I'm admitting nothing. Let me ask you something. Is that shirt you're wearing one hundred percent cotton?"

135

"No . . ."

"You're goddamn right it isn't. We probably made fifty or sixty percent of that shirt. You want to talk chemicals? You're wearing 'em!"

"I don't see what that has to do with anything."

"It has to do with everything. You and Annie and everybody else can blame the chemical industry for America's environmental ills. But you conveniently ignore the major accomplice: the American public. A public that wears clothes made of synthetic fibers. A public that drives cars made of plastic parts. A public that eats food raised in chemicals, and wrapped for sale in chemicals. A public whose collective ass rests on plastic furniture. A public that includes people like Annie, who buys her 'No Nukes' and 'Live AID' albums ignoring the fact that records are a petrochemical by-product, then plays them on her stereo, thanks to nuclear-generated electricity."

"Now who sounds like a goddamn pamphlet?"

"Hey, I'm not ashamed to be working in the chemical industry. I think we provide a service, *many* services, the public wants. Needs. *Demands.* The chemical industry's *booming,* pal — recessions don't touch us. $133 billion last year. And next year, who knows?"

"Kind of like cancer statistics."

"Don't be an asshole. We don't live in a zero-risk environment. Never have and never will. And if we tried, there'd be no creativity. No scientific advancement. Innovation would be stifled."

"Let me see if I got this straight. If we want to keep listening to 'No Nukes' albums and Willie Nelson, we need to accept the fact that the environment may get fucked over."

"Crane, it's bad business to market hazardous products; it's good business to market safe products. Have you been around Annie so long that the simple logic

136

of that is lost on you? It's crazy for you or Annie or anyone to think the chemical industry is going to make a practice out of being irresponsible. Just to make an extra buck or two. It just ain't necessary, Crane. It ain't good business."

Crane sipped the Pepsi. His first sip. It was warm now. "Then why do some Kemco plants still make Agent Orange?"

"You mean 2,4,5-T."

"Yes. They're not dumping it on Vietnam anymore. But it's still being dumped on American forests."

"Of course it is. It's an established tool of forest production."

"It's got dioxin in it."

"Yes."

"Dioxin is only the worst foul fucking thing in the world, Patrick. It causes cancer. Birth defects. You name it. Good shit, as a retread '60s doper like you might put it."

"Accusations like that have been leveled at 2,4,5-T for years, but the government has yet to ban it. And we believe it provides an important service."

"Sure."

"I'm surprised you haven't realized yet how one-sided Annie's research is, Crane. How conveniently she ignores the facts she doesn't like. The U.S. Forest Service did a study on the use of 2,4,5-T in the Northwest, and found that discontinuing the use of the herbicide would have an economic impact of several hundred million dollars on Oregon alone. That's jobs that would be lost, Crane. Families that would suffer. All because without that herbicide, the brush would come in and take over what would've been a healthy new forest. Did Annie's research tell you that?"

Crane said nothing.

"You know, Crane, these well-meaning leftists are

137

engaging in what you could call 'chemical McCarthyism.' The chemical industry makes such an easy target. The public doesn't understand the science, the technology involved. The environmentalist types come along and spout some half-truths and whole lies, all because of an irrational, unscientific distrust of anything that isn't 'natural,' that might tamper with Nature in a way God didn't intend, only most of them don't believe in God, so go figure. I don't know. I'm just a guy trying to make an honest buck. I never hurt anybody."

Crane said nothing.

"I'll get somebody to take you home," Patrick said. No more smiles. No more rhetoric. He seemed tired.

"I'm sorry about Mary Beth," he said. "I really am."

The hell of it was Crane believed him.

Crane was sitting on the couch in Boone's house, watching a late movie without paying attention to it, when Boone got home.

He could tell things hadn't gone well for her. Her face looked tired. Her hair was messy, greasy. But she still looked pretty, as she gave him a weary smile and came over and joined him on the couch.

"I could use a kiss," she said.

"Who couldn't?" he said, smiling a little, kissing her.

He put an arm around her and she cuddled against him.

"How did you and Billy get along?" she asked.

"Swell. He spoke twice: 'What's for supper?' and 'I'll stay up as late as I want.'"

Tired as she was, she managed a smile. "You cooked for him?"

"Sure. Another of my specialties: frozen pizza."

"When did he get to bed?"

"Half an hour ago."

"He's got school tomorrow."

"That's his problem."

"Well, you didn't fare much worse than most of his baby-sitters."

"How did you fare?"

"With the 'Hazardous Waste Strike Force,' you mean?"

"Yeah."

"Don't ask."

He didn't say anything for a while; neither did she. Then she rose and said, "How about some wine?"

"Sounds almost as good as another kiss."

"Doesn't it?"

She went away for a few minutes, came back with a bottle of red wine and some wineglasses. She poured. They drank. They kissed again. Then she got thoughtful.

"It was like talking to you," she said.

"What was?"

"Telling my story to the Task Force guy. His name was Hart. Sidney Hart. He was a nice guy, about my age. A special investigator assigned through the state police to the Task Force. He spent hours listening to me."

"What did he say?"

"Like I said, it was like talking to you. He was interested in what I had to say, polite, but skeptical. He said he'd heard rumors about Kemco, but that the company had never been caught in a major violation. He questioned what we'd really seen last night. Yes, it's suspicious for trucks to haul waste to a landfill at night; but it isn't necessarily illegal."

"What about the manifest system? What if Kemco didn't report the dumping"

"Then it's just our word against Kemco's that any dumping took place at all. We didn't even write down the license number of the fucking truck, 'cause we thought we had it on film."

"It was New Jersey plates."

"But you don't remember the number, do you? Me either. So all we've got is our story, and who's going

140

to take us seriously? Who are you, but the fiancé of a woman you think Kemco killed? And who am I, but the disgruntled ex-wife of a Kemco executive, out for blood, right? What kind of credibility does that give us?"

"That's what Patrick said."

"Patrick?"

"Yeah. I talked to him this afternoon."

"You talked to Patrick?"

Crane told her about the Kemco car stopping for him, about going out there and spending half an hour with her ex-husband.

"I can't say he struck me as . . . a monster or anything." Crane said.

She moved away from him on the couch, just a little. "How *did* he strike you?"

"I didn't exactly like him. And I can understand why you couldn't put up with his attitudes. But I find it difficult to believe he's in any way involved with Mary Beth's death."

"He *must* be."

"You really think your ex-husband is a murderer? Your son's father?"

"Patrick is . . . it's possible."

"You can't say it, can you? The guy's selfish and self-centered and I think he'd do a lot of shady things if his bosses asked him to . . . like maybe pay off some midnight haulers in cash . . . but not murder. I just don't buy it. And I don't think you do either, if you'd be honest with yourself."

"It's a criminal conspiracy, Crane. It's Watergate. It's something that got out of control, that people got caught up in. And Patrick was one of them."

"It's not Watergate, Boone, and even if it was, I don't remember anybody getting killed over Watergate."

"Who really knows?"

"Oh Christ. Let's not sing the Paranoid Conspiracy Nut Blues again."

"What do *you* think happened to Mary Beth, then? You think she killed herself?"

Crane put down the wineglass. He looked at Boone. Their eyes locked.

"Yes," he said.

"Crane . . ."

"I don't like it. I don't *want* to believe it. But yes. I think she killed herself."

"No . . ."

"Yes."

"What about all the other 'suicides'?"

"They were suicides. I talked with Mrs. Meyer today. She's fiercely loyal to Kemco; feels they've done right by her. I found something out from her that you didn't, when you interviewed her for your book: her husband had a long history of mental illness. He had very deep emotional problems that didn't have a goddamn thing to do with Kemco."

"Ten times the national suicide rate, Crane!"

"That's just a fluke. I talked with Mrs. Price, too, and *her* husband was an emotionally disturbed person, headed for a breakdown. Headed for suicide."

"Crane, Mary Beth knew something. It's Karen Silkwood all over again. She was killed because she had something on Kemco."

"What did she know? About the midnight dumping? *We* know about it. We're still alive."

"What did you say to Patrick about last night?"

"Nothing."

"Does he know about it?"

"If he does, he didn't indicate it."

"Maybe they don't know about us. Maybe we weren't seen last night."

"Fine, but that shoots your theory about the truckers stealing your camera, doesn't it? You can't have it both ways. To steal it, they'd have to know about us. And if they know about us, our lives are in danger."

"Well maybe our lives *are* in danger."

"I don't think so. If a decision had been made to add us to the suicide rate, why would Patrick bother having me out for a talk this afternoon? No, Boone, it doesn't make sense. It's all very confusing, but there's nothing sinister going on here at all."

"Dumping hazardous waste in an ordinary household dump, in the middle of the night, isn't sinister?"

"It's criminal, Boone. You're right about that. I don't doubt for a moment that Kemco is a criminally irresponsible company, but . . ."

"A baby girl with a cleft palate, Crane. That sinister enough for you? Liver disorders? Nervous conditions? High miscarriage rates? High cancer rates? Any of that strike you as sinister?"

"It strikes me as depressing, and since you exposed Mary Beth to your crusade, as you have me, it's no wonder she was depressed, living in the house where her father died of cancer, living in a house where across the hall little Brucie in his crib paws the air with no hands, and you come along and fill her with your bleak vision of a chemically contaminated America, it's no *wonder* she slashed her wrists."

Boone sat quietly for a moment, staring into the redness in her wineglass. Without looking at Crane, she said, "So. Finally it comes around to this."

"To what?"

"To it being my fault. Mary Beth's suicide."

"No. You're wrong. I don't blame you."

"You're just too fucking generous, Crane."

"You're right about one thing: it *was* suicide. I believe that now. I don't like it. But I believe it."

143

"Then maybe you better go back to Iowa."

"Maybe I better."

She rose, slamming her glass down on the coffee table, splashing wine. She looked down at him, giving him a cold, sarcastic look, the likes of which he hadn't seen from her since their early, off-on-the-wrong-foot moments together.

"Go back to school, Crane. Learn something."

"All right."

She walked toward the stairs.

"Boone . . ."

She stopped; her back was to him.

"Is this the way it has to be?"

"I don't know," she said. There was no sarcasm in her voice, now. It sounded very small.

"Your book, Boone. It's good. It's more than good: it's important. What you say about Agent Orange and its effect on the Vietnam vets. Your study into the effects of Kemco on its workers and their families, their town. The midnight hauling story. *That* can go into the book. Our staking out the Kemco plant; your camera maybe being stolen, that can be a nice ambiguous touch . . . all of it. You've got enough, Boone. You don't have your smoking gun, exactly, but what you've got is good. But Mary Beth killed herself, and so did the others. Accept it. Leave it behind. And go ahead and finish your book and publish it and tell your story on Donahue. Wake America up. But be a journalist. Don't be a conspiracy nut."

Without turning, she said, "I'm going to bed."

"I still believe in what you're doing."

"That's nice."

"Boone."

"What?"

"What about this morning?"

"What about it?"

144

"Why don't you come over here and sit down with me."

"And what?"

"And we won't talk anymore."

"And it'll be just like this morning? At the motel?"

"I hope it will."

"Your timing sucks, Crane."

She went upstairs.

He sat on the couch all night, without sleeping.

In the morning she drove him to where he could catch the bus that would take him to the airport. She didn't say anything the whole way, but just as he got out, she leaned over and kissed him, and then drove away and left him.

The Mill was a late '60s time warp. The booths were displaced church pews; stained-glass panels hung behind the bar; a folksinger was doing something by Phil Ochs. During the folksinger's break, somebody put money in a jukebox that still had "Big Yellow Taxi" on it and when something by Sting came out, it seemed like a mistake. A waitress in sweater and jeans took an order, then spoke to her black boyfriend for five minutes before turning it in. Two guys with ponytails and facial hair sat facing each other, leaning across one of the tables scattered between the pews and the bar, making a conspiracy out of a dope deal as if anyone still cared, saying "man" a lot, like it was fifteen years ago in California, and not today in Iowa City.

Crane hated the Mill.

But his friend Roger Beatty and Roger's girl Judy had talked him into coming along. The food at the Mill was good, particularly the antipasto salad, and afterwards they would go to the Bijou Theater for a John Wayne movie, *The Searchers*. Roger said it was a great movie, so Crane had consented to come. He hadn't been out much since he got back from Greenwood. He hadn't been out at all, really. Maybe it was time he did.

Roger was explaining some things about the movie

to Judy, who was listening patiently, or pretending to. Judy usually didn't go in for these old movies, and Crane wondered why she was here.

Judy was a thin, pretty girl with a short dark cap of hair and dark blue eyes with long lashes; she gave Crane a slow sideways look, while Roger babbled ("doorways in the film represent civilization") and gestured with both hands, the eyes behind his thick glasses lost in themselves.

Their antipasto salads came, and they ate, Roger continuing his critique of the film they would be seeing, Crane beginning to feel uncomfortable with Judy's eyes on him. He knew her well enough to know she wasn't putting the make on him. So why was she staring?

Finally Roger, who liked food even more than films, shut up and ate.

Judy said, "I'm glad you're getting out tonight, Crane. You needed it."

He managed a smile. "Who needs to see a movie, with Roger here to tell it to you."

Roger looked up from his salad. "I was just giving you some background."

"Like the ending," Judy asked, with a not unpleasant smirk.

Crane smiled at them and said, "It's nice of you guys to ask me along. I haven't been doing much lately except study."

"Not that it shows," Roger said.

Crane shrugged. "I missed a few deadlines."

"Yeah, and had some pieces rejected."

"What's the problem, Crane?" Judy asked.

Roger said, "He's going to lose his spot on the *Daily Iowan*, is the problem. You know how many journalism majors are lined up in back of you, Crane, wanting on that staff?"

"Just all of them," Crane said.

"So what's the problem?" Judy asked again.

"He's still got his head back in New Jersey," Roger said.

Crane didn't say anything.

Their waitress brought the food: Roger had a small pizza, Judy spaghetti, Crane vegetarian lasagna.

Roger and Judy began to eat.

Crane poked at his food with his fork.

"Why don't you call her?" Roger said.

"Roger. Please."

"I know you don't want to talk about it in front of Judy, but I already told her all about it."

"Thanks, Roger. Confiding in you is like taking out an ad."

Judy said, "Why *don't* you call her, Crane? See what's been happening? It's been a month."

"Five weeks," he said.

"And you wrote her one letter and she didn't answer it. That isn't much of an effort to get through to her."

"Who says I should try to get through to her?"

"Nobody," Roger said. "But you better start getting with it."

"Getting with it."

"Yeah. Do your work. Have some fun. You know. Live a little."

"Can I quote you?"

"Go ahead. Maybe if you use my stuff you won't get rejected."

Judy touched Roger's arm and gave him a sharp look. Roger shook his head and took his frustration out on a slice of pizza.

Crane took a bit of lasagna: it was cold; he ate it anyway.

After the meal they had some wine and Crane said,

"I know you two are trying to help, and I appreciate it. Really. I'm glad to be out among the living again. But your advice . . . well, it's just that I've been over all of this in my own head so many times that . . ."

"Do you still think about Mary Beth?" Judy asked.

"Of course I still think about Mary Beth! I still sleep in the same bed I slept in with her, damnit."

"From the way you just snapped at me," Judy said, giving him her slow, long-lashed look, "I'd say you've got a bad case of the guilts."

"The guilts."

"That's right. You went to your girlfriend's funeral, and you met this Boone and went home with her. And you feel guilty about it, and that's why you haven't made any real effort to get back in touch with her. You're punishing yourself."

"Judy, I know you mean well, but you just don't understand."

"Maybe not. But I'd like to. So would Roger."

Crane didn't say anything.

Neither did Judy or Roger, for a few long minutes.

Then Crane said, "All right, maybe I do feel guilty about Boone and me, getting together so soon after what happened to Mary Beth . . ." He shook his head. "But that isn't what . . . you see, what came between Boone and me was the goddamn Kemco thing. I couldn't get her to accept that Mary Beth's death was really suicide."

"It probably was," Judy said, nodding.

"What probably was?"

"Mary Beth's death. It probably was suicide. I agree with you."

"That sounds like an expert opinion."

"Well, maybe it is. When Roger started talking about all this, telling me some of what you told him about the Kemco situation, I did some reading up.

152

They make Agent Orange at that plant, don't they?"

"Yes."

"So we're talking dioxin, among other goodies."

"That's right."

"Keep it simple," Roger interrupted, between sips of red wine. "We're not all science majors, here, you know."

Judy said, "Three *ounces* of dioxin in the New York City water supply could wipe out the city's population. At Love Canal—you've heard of Love Canal, Roger? At Love Canal, they buried 130 *pounds* of the stuff."

"Judas," Roger said.

"Here's the point, Crane," Judy continued. "In addition to being one terrific carcinogen, and the bearer of such glad tidings as liver disease and miscarriages, dioxin can cause *psychological* disturbances. And what *is* a suicide victim, other than a psychologically disturbed person?"

"Very few well-balanced folks kill themselves," Roger conceded.

Crane leaned forward. "Then the depressed state Mary Beth and the other suicides were in might've been brought on . . . or anyway, amplified . . . by chemicals they'd been exposed to?"

"Why not?" Judy asked. "They all worked at that plant, didn't they? Now if a *non*-Kemco employee in Greenwood committed suicide—particularly somebody who'd been asking embarassing questions around town, like you had—*that* would be suspicious. Then I'd be inclined to agree with your Boone that people were being murdered to look like suicide."

"There's something I don't get," Roger said. "The Kemco plant is twenty miles or so from Greenwood, right? Then why the high rate of illnesses and such among the families of employees? The families aren't

153

directly exposed to any Kemco pollution."

"Yet the wives and husbands and children *are* affected," Judy said, nodding.

"Skin rashes for the kids," Crane said, "miscarriages for mom, loss of sex drive for dad, fun for the whole family."

"It really does sound like Love Canal," Judy said. "Same kinds of things were reported there, only the reason for it all became obvious, when corroded waste drums started to break up through the ground in backyards. Did you know one backyard swimming pool popped up right out of its foundation? Floating in chemical shit. And people had pools of this stuff, oozing, bubbling up in their basements."

"Thanks for waiting till after dinner to get into this," Roger said, pale.

"The government moved a lot of people out of Love Canal," Judy went on, "but some had to stay behind. Out of less than 200 homes, bordering on the condemned area, there were twenty-some birth defects, thirty-some miscarriages, forty-some cases of respiratory disease. I don't know the exact figures, of course, but you get the idea."

Roger pointed a thumb at her and said, "She doesn't know the exact figures, of course."

"I do know that there were something like twenty nervous breakdowns and three or four suicides . . . *suicides,* Crane."

"In less than 200 homes?"

"That's right. Wrap the national suicide rate around *that* one."

"Maybe . . . maybe I should talk to Boone again."

"Of course you should," Roger said. "Go use the pay phone."

"It's long distance . . ."

Roger grinned and pulled a roll of quarters out from

somewhere. "Here you go," he said; he rolled the roll toward Crane, who caught it.

"Why do I get the feeling I've been set up?" Crane said, smiling at his two friends; they shrugged and smiled back at him as he got out of the booth.

He went to the phone on the wall over by the rest rooms and made the station-to-station call. He let it ring a dozen times. It was a big house, after all. No answer. He called information and got another number. He made the second station-to-station call, and on the third ring, Mary Beth's mother answered.

He didn't identify himself; he just asked to speak to Laurie. Mary Beth's mother said she would put Laurie on.

"Hello?"

"Laurie? This is Crane."

"Crane! Why you must be calling about Boone."

"Why, yes . . ."

"Who told you? Did her husband call you about it?"

"About what?"

"About Boone. About her taking all those pills. Last I heard, she was still in a coma."

"Are you sure you'll be all right?" Laurie asked.

"Yes," Crane said.

It was dusk. The trees lining Boone's street were skeletal, abstract shapes; the ground was white and brown, patches of leaves showing through the light covering of snow. It looked peaceful to Crane. Peaceful like death.

"I'd rather you came and stayed with us," Laurie said. "Mother would like you to. We have the room."

"No, thank you, Laurie, but I could never stay in that house." He didn't look at her as he said this; he'd been with her since late this morning, when she picked him up at the airport, but he hadn't looked at her much. She was still too much a plumper, slightly older version of Mary Beth for him to be comfortable looking at her.

"You'll be staying at the motel, then?"

"Yes."

"For how long?"

"As long as it takes."

"Crane, she could be in that coma for a year."

"Or forever."

"Or forever. The doctor as much as said so. And if she does wake up, she could . . ."

"Be a vegetable. He as much as said that, too."

"Not necessarily. He did say they got to her within the first hour. He said that was encouraging."

"Somewhat encouraging."

"Somewhat encouraging, he said. But you can't stay around here forever, waiting for Boone to wake up. It's crazy."

Crazy. Crazy was Boone in Intensive Care with tubes in her. That was what crazy was.

"Laurie, I want to thank you for everything. Picking me up at the airport, driving me to the hospital at Fair View, sticking around till I talked to the doctor. Everything."

"It's all right, Crane. You were almost my brother-in-law, remember?" She smiled at him, a little.

"I remember." He couldn't find a smile to give her back. He tried, but it wasn't there.

"You're sure you want out here? Not at the motel?"

"This is where I want out."

There were lights on in Boone's house, in the downstairs. Two cars were parked at the curb: an MGB and Boone's yellow Datsun. There was snow on the Datsun. Laurie was double-parked with the motor running.

Though they'd been together for some hours, he and Laurie hadn't said much. It had seemed to him that Laurie had tried several times to say something and hadn't been able to. He glanced at her now, as he opened the car door to get out, and realized she was trying one last time.

"Crane . . . you and Boone. You must've gotten . . . close."

He closed the door and settled back in the seat.

"Laurie," he said, "I love her. That doesn't take anything away from how I felt about Mary Beth. I still love Mary Beth, and she's dead. And now Boone, and she's in a coma. I love them both, and I let them both

157

down, or they wouldn't be where they are right now."

"Don't say that."

He shrugged.

Laurie was struggling again.

Crane said, "Say what's on your mind. Go on."

"It's just . . . you told me you were leaving town . . . told mother the same thing . . . then you move in with Boone. You never called or anything, saying you'd changed your mind about going or anything. But I knew you were still in Greenwood, and with Boone. This is a small town, Crane, in case you haven't noticed. Word gets around."

She had tried to keep the resentment out of her voice, but it was there.

He said. "I didn't want to bother you and your mother again. I didn't want to worry either of you with my suspicions."

"Suspicions?"

"About Mary Beth's death."

"Is that why you were asking questions around town?"

"Yes."

"Then, what? You think Mary Beth was, what? Murdered?"

"Yes. I'd convinced myself that it was something else, but now . . ."

"Now Boone attempts suicide, too, and that's just one too many suicides for you to swallow. Sorry. Poor choice of words."

"Not so poor. You said this was a small town. Hasn't anybody in Greenwood noticed that suicide is going around like the mumps?"

"Of course."

"And?"

"People think it's strange."

"And?"

"They just think it's strange. Not suspicious. Just strange."

"What do you think?"

"I think it's suspicious. But I don't know what you're going to do about it, if that's why you're staying around."

"Well, I have no plans for suicide . . . so if I turn up some morning sleeping under an exhaust pipe, it wasn't my idea, if anybody asks."

"You're scaring me."

"I'm sorry. I didn't mean to get into this."

"Crane."

"Yes?"

"What are you going to do?"

"Nothing. Go home to your kid, Laurie. I appreciate you picking me up, driving me around today."

He got out of the car.

"If you want a ride to Fair View to see Boone tomorrow, or any day," Laurie said, "just call. Mom can sit with Brucie."

"Thanks."

"Maybe she'll wake up, Crane."

"Maybe she will."

Laurie drove off.

He turned and looked at Boone's house. One of the upstairs windows was boarded up. Odd.

He knocked on the door.

Billy answered. He seemed to have grown a little.

"Hello, Billy."

Billy looked at Crane through squinty eyes, not recognizing him at first. When recognition came, it was a wave of disgust over the six year old's face. He turned away and yelled, "Daddy!" and disappeared.

A moment later, like a special effect in a movie, the young version of Billy was replaced by the older one: Patrick. He was in a white shirt with his collar and

159

tie loose. His eyes behind the wire frames showed confusion, though it was clear he, unlike Billy, knew Crane immediately.

"What are you doing here?" he asked, without hostility.

"I could ask you the same thing," Crane said.

Patrick shrugged. "I moved in the day after it happened. That's, what? Two days ago. Come in, come in."

Crane did, but they did not advance to the living room; they stayed right in the entryway, standing awkwardly, like strangers thrown together at a cocktail party. Or a wake.

"Don't you have an apartment in Fair View?" Crane said.

"Yes. And I considered staying there, to be closer to Annie. Not that I could do anything for her at this point."

"Why move in here?"

"Greenwood's where Billy goes to school. Fair View is thirty miles from here. So I moved in to be with Billy. So his life wouldn't be too disrupted."

Billy was sitting on the floor in the next room watching TV.

"It's hell to have your life disrupted," Crane said.

"Look. I have had some rough damn days, here, you know. Yesterday I didn't get into work at all. Today at work I had to make up for yesterday. I haven't even had a chance to get back to the apartment to move some of my stuff here. I just packed a bag and came, to be with my son."

"What about your wife?"

"My ex-wife. A disturbed, irrational woman. I can't say I feel much love for her anymore. The only thing I feel is sorry for her."

"Sorry for her."

160

"Crane, what are you doing here? Somebody called you about Annie, and you came, but there's nothing for you to do here. She's in a coma."

"I noticed."

"You saw her, then."

"I saw her."

Patrick swallowed. Suddenly his face looked white, long. "Poor Annie," he said. Looking at the floor.

"Who did it?"

"Who did what?"

"Shoved those pills in her."

"Keep your voice down."

"It's down. Who did it?"

"She did it."

"She took those pills herself? Voluntarily?"

"She was irrational! Troubled."

"She was almost murdered is what she was, and I want to know *your* part in it."

"My part . . . ? Get the fuck out of here."

"You tell me first. Who did this? You don't have the balls to do it yourself, Patrick. Who did it?"

Patrick spoke through his teeth. "She did it. You can't stuff a bottle of barbiturates down somebody's throat. They take it because they want to."

"What was she doing with barbiturates? I know how she feels about drugs."

"Didn't you talk to the doctor? She had a prescription. They were to help her sleep."

"Why would she be having trouble sleeping?"

"Maybe it was because she and her new boyfriend had a spat, and he ran out on her."

"Fuck you, Patrick."

"Get out of my house."

"This isn't your house. We both know whose house it is."

"Get out!"

161

Billy called from the other room. "Daddy?"

"It's okay, Billy," Patrick said. Then to Crane, no sarcasm, no anger: "Please. Just go."

"I'll go. For now."

Crane was halfway down the front walk when he heard Patrick's voice behind him: "I hope to God Annie comes out of it. Then she can tell you herself what happened."

Crane kept walking.

"Crane, I wouldn't hurt my son's mother. I wouldn't do that."

That stopped him: he felt himself believing Patrick again. Goddamnit.

"What really happened, Patrick?" he said, turning.

"I told you. I told you. I fucking *told* you! She was troubled. She wasn't herself. You left town, and . . ."

He went to Patrick. "And what?"

"Well. In a way maybe I did contribute to it."

"What are you talking about?"

"I petitioned the court for custody of my son."

"You what?"

"I wanted Billy and I thought I could get him. Annie wouldn't have come off too good in court, a woman who'd made no effort to get a job, instead spending all her energies trying to destroy me and the company that employed me and, indirectly, fed her and my son. Also, she'd had a man living in the house with her — you — and that wouldn't have looked good for her."

"When was this?"

"Last week."

"You'd just served the papers on her? You hadn't gone to court yet?"

"That's right."

"And so she took a bottle of sleeping pills? Get serious."

"That was just a small part of it."

162

"Was it."

"Yes."

"What was the big part?"

"Well, the fire, of course."

"What fire?"

"Didn't you know? Four days ago, there was a fire here. Neither she nor Billy were in the house. Some rooms upstairs were pretty badly burned; her study was gutted. The fire department, such as it is, stopped it from spreading thoughout the house. We were lucky."

"Her study was gutted?"

"Yes. That's what set her off, Crane, I'm sure."

Crane looked up at the boarded-over window on the second floor.

"Her book," Patrick was saying, "her research files. Everything. All of it. Burned up in the fire."

It was hard to tell where the overcast day ended and the smoke from Kemco began. The buildings with their aqua plastic walls and intertwining pipes seemed to suit this bleak, cold afternoon. So did the snow-flecked empty field across the way, that immense balding dandruff-spotted scalp, farmland where no one dared grow anything.

He thanked Laurie for driving him out there. She said she could wait for him and drive him back when he was done, but he told her no, he was quite sure he could find a ride back.

They'd been to see Boone again. The doctor had let him sit in the room with Boone, for about an hour. She looked pale. A little thin. But still very pretty. She seemed to be asleep. He found himself thinking of Mary Beth. He remembered the conscious decision he'd made at the funeral not to look at her as she lay in her casket. If Boone died, he knew he would see her this way, forever: forever in a coma. He knew it and hated it. But he would be here. Even as she deteriorated physically, getting thinner, thinner. Intravenous feeding could keep her alive; but she'd still seem to waste away. But he would be here. Every day, as long as it took. Sitting in her room. Till she woke up. Or not.

Soon he'd have to deal with his parents. He hadn't called them before he left; he wasn't up to arguing about this. He'd written them a letter, telling them he was dropping out for the semester and going back to Greenwood. They knew nothing about him and Boone; they wouldn't begin to understand what this was about. Eventually he would have to tell them. Eventually he would have to tell them he'd drawn out from his bank account all of the school money he worked for this summer, to live on here.

But that would have to wait.

Boone came first.

Boone, and Kemco.

He walked into the building that housed the executive offices; the receptionist looked at him from her window in her wall and asked him who he was there to see. He told her Mr. Boone was expecting him. Which was nonsense, but Patrick wasn't likely to turn him away, either.

He sat down on one of the plaid-upholstered couches. He noticed that the quote from the founder ("Industry is people") was hanging crooked in its frame, above the other couch. He got up and straightened it and sat down again.

Patrick was in his shirt-sleeves with a dark blue tie, and slacks and face about the same color gray. He stood on the other side of the turnstile that separated the reception area and hallway, keeping it between him and Crane.

"What do you want?" he said. His voice seemed strained. The eyes behind the wire frames blinked.

Crane stood. He put on a small smile. "Just want to talk, Patrick."

"We talked last night."

"Patrick. Please. I came to apologize, in a way. Could we go to your office?"

Patrick studied Crane for what seemed like a long time. The smile made Crane's face hurt, but he kept it on.

Finally Patrick motioned at him to come on, nodding at the receptionist that it was okay. Crane went through the turnstile and followed Patrick down the long, rather wide hall.

Patrick told his secretary to hold all calls and closed the door behind Crane and himself. He sat behind his desk. Folded his hands. Crane took a chair and sat across from him, not bothering to smile anymore, but keeping a neutral expression.

"I'll go to the police," Patrick said.

"What are you talking about, Patrick?"

"I'm just someone trying to make a living, trying to raise a son. I can't take this harrassment. I won't be harrassed, Crane!"

"Patrick. I told you. I came to apologize."

"Right."

"I mean it. I've been out of line. Finding out what happened to Boone threw me out of whack. You can understand that."

Patrick nodded, slowly, still not quite buying it.

"Surely, you admit some strange things have been happening," Crane said.

"Yes. I admit that."

"Like the fire. Like the suicides."

"I told you last night, the police and fire department agreed that there was no evidence of arson."

"I know you did. But you can understand why I can't get too worked up over the opinions of Greenwood's Finest."

Patrick shrugged. "Crane, if I believed that that had been arson, I'd be the first to complain."

"Well, sure. I can see how you'd want to do that.

I can see where a complaint might be in order."

Patrick shifted in his swivel chair, studying Crane, looking for sarcasm, not quite finding it.

Crane said, "I came here to tell you I'm leaving Greenwood."

"You are?"

"That's right. I'll send you my address and phone number, in Iowa City. I'd appreciate it if you'd keep me posted, where Boone's concerned."

Patrick lifted his eyebrows. "Well, of course. Why not."

"I know it must've been a blow to Boone to lose all her research materials. To have her entire manuscript, months of work, go up in smoke."

He nodded. "She was devastated. As I told you last night, I'm convinced that's why she did what she did."

"Took those pills."

"Yes."

"At least there's one encouraging note."

"Yes?"

"When we spoke, you and I, five weeks ago, you said Kemco itself was concerned about some of Boone's findings . . . the high incidence of certain illnesses among employees and their families, for example. You said Kemco would be doing its own study into the matter."

"That's right."

"How's it coming along?"

"Well. It's in the beginning stages. The home office in St. Louis is putting it in motion, I'm told."

"I'm glad to hear it."

"Then you're really going, Crane?"

"Yes. There's nothing for me, here. I have to get back to Iowa and hit the old books."

Patrick rose. "Well, then. I'll show you out."

167

Crane smiled again. "No need. I know the way."
He extended his hand to Patrick. "Sorry about our mis-
understandings, Patrick. They shook hands across the
desk.

Patrick smiled and said, "We might've been friends,
under different circumstances."

Crane kept the smile going. "Who knows?" he said.

He left Patrick's office. He glanced back and saw
Patrick had followed him out in the hall, watching him.
Crane waved, smiled, went into the room marked
MEN.

He went into one of the stalls and sat; he kept his
pants up. He sat and looked at his watch. When five
minutes had passed he left the stall. He peeked out
in the hall. No Patrick.

Down the Hall from Patrick's office was a door that
said PLANT MANAGER.

Crane opened it.

The secretary looked up, a woman in her late thir-
ties with short dark hair and glasses and a nice smile.
"Do you have an appointment with Mr. Johnson?"

"I don't need one," Crane said, and opened the door,
at the left, which said WALTER JOHNSON, PLANT
MANAGER.

Johnson was a thickset man about fifty, with wiry
brown hair going gray, a mustache, wire-rim glasses.
He was in his shirt-sleeves and a red-and-blue striped
tie, with some work on his desk and a phone receiver
to his ear.

At first he smiled, just hearing the door open, not
looking at Crane, assuming it was his secretary or someone with something important his secretary had sent
on in; but the smile was momentary, turning to confusion on seeing someone he didn't know barge in, turning to irritation that would've turned to anger if Crane
hadn't slammed a fist on the man's desk, upsetting

168

papers, spilling a half a cup of coffee, rattling the desk itself, turning Johnson's expression to one of fear.

"Hang up the fucking phone," Crane said.

Johnson said, "Excuse me," into the receiver, softly, hung up.

The secretary was behind Crane, having come in on his heels, and Johnson motioned to her to leave and she did.

"Who are you?" Johnson said.

"Crane."

"Is that supposed to mean something to me?"

"I think so."

"Well it doesn't."

"How about Anne Boone? Does that mean anything?" He then listed the other "suicides": Woll, Meyer, Price, Mary Beth.

Johnson said, "I know those names. All of them worked for us, except Mrs. Boone. And Mrs. Boone's husband is in our employ."

"I know all about Patrick being in your employ. And I know all about what you people have been up to. Everything from dumping hazardous wastes in household dumps to unsafe working conditions at the plant; I know about your arson, I know about your phony suicides, which is to say murder."

Johnson said nothing. He was looking Crane over, nervously, possibly wondering if Crane had a gun.

Crane pointed a finger at him. "I know. I know all about everything. Burning Boone's book won't stop a goddamn thing. I'm going to have your corporate asses. I'm taking what I have to the Hazardous Waste Strike Force, and to the media and . . ."

The door opened behind him. Two armed security guards, one of them a woman, came in.

"Hold him!" Johnson shouted. He was standing behind the desk, now, shaking, furious, not quite over being afraid. "Hold him while I call the police."

Patrick came in the room. He looked briefly dismayed, then was all business.

"Walt," he said. "Let me have a word with you."

The guards escorted Crane into the outer office. They stood. He sat. Voices within Johnson's office argued.

A few minutes later Patrick came back out.

"Do you have a car here?" Patrick asked Crane.

"No," Crane said.

"I'll drive you."

"What about the police?"

"I've convinced Mr. Johnson not to bring them in. Next time, don't expect me to bail you out, Crane."

"What would I do without you."

"Are you going to cause any more trouble?"

"Not today."

For the first ten minutes of the ride back to Greenwood, Patrick said nothing; he just drove, quietly fuming, like the Kemco plant.

Then he laughed; it sounded harsh. "I believed you," he said.

"Don't be bitter, " Crane said. "I've fallen for your bullshit, on occasion."

"What was the purpose of all that back there, Crane?"

Crane shrugged.

"Are you flipping, or what?"

Crane didn't say anything.

Patrick shoved an Eagles tape into his dash and turned it up loud. At least it wasn't Willie Nelson, Crane thought. He found Patrick's little sports car comfortable enough. He settled back.

When Patrick pulled up at the motel, he said, "You better do what you said you were going to do: leave town."

"Thanks for the lift," Crane said. He got out.

170

Patrick shook his head and drove off.

In his motel room, Crane made some phone calls. Then he walked to the pizza place downtown and ate. By the time he finished, it was dark. A light snow was falling. He walked to Boone's house. Patrick's car, the MGB, was in front. So was Boone's Datsun, still covered with snow. No one had touched it since her "suicide attempt," he'd bet.

There was no one around; the street light was still out. He felt fairly safe going over to the Datsun and seeing if it was locked. It wasn't.

He opened the glove compartment. Reached his hand in. Felt the coldness: the gun was still in there.

He put it in his belt, shut the door of the Datsun and walked back to the motel room.

Kids were bundled in their winter clothes as they left the grade school, walking into the blowing snow. Some of them got onto the waiting buses; other paused impatiently till the crossing guards let them trudge homeward. None of them were playing or fooling around, today: the wind had teeth and they wanted to get away from it.

Crane liked the way it felt on his face, the wind, the snow. There was some ice mixed in with it, and it whipped him, like a sandstorm. He stood in the playground shivering, hands in the pockets of his light summer jacket.

Billy was wearing a parka. He and two other boys passed right by Crane. Billy didn't look at him. Crane wasn't sure if he was being ignored or just hadn't been seen. He did know that he had the odd urge to grab the boy, hug him, hold him to him. The feeling lasted only a moment, and Crane didn't understand it: he genuinely disliked the kid.

Over to the left, on the same side of the street as the playground, a local cop car was parked, its motor running. The officer he'd talked to in the candy shop, five weeks ago, was sitting in it, alone, keeping an eye on the kids. Thin, dark-complected guy named, what was it? Turner. Officer Turner.

He walked over and knocked on the driver's window and Turner rolled it down. He said, "Yes? Got a problem?" Turner's breath was visible, like pollution.

"Just saying hello," Crane said. "We spoke a month or so ago, about my fiancée's death."

"Oh, sure. Crane, isn't it? How's it going?"

"Not bad. How about you?"

"Can't complain."

"Kind of slow in Greenwood these days?"

"Yeah. Kind of. You know how it is."

"Sure. You probably haven't had a suicide since Thursday."

"What?"

"Nice seeing you, officer. Keep up the good work."

He turned his back on Turner and walked across the street and into the school. It was pretty well cleared out, very few kids, just a few teachers.

He quickly found the cafeteria. It was a big white room full of long tables with no one in it, except Mrs. Price, who was sitting drinking a cup of coffee. She looked tired; she seemed to have lost some weight. She was wearing a gray dress and little makeup and her red hair was rather mussed.

"Mr. Crane," she said, with a perfunctory smile, getting up, sitting back down. "There's coffee over there. Help yourself."

He did.

He came back and sat down and sipped black coffee from a Styrofoam cup. Slipped off his wet jacket and draped it over the back of his chair.

"Well," she said. Hands folded. "You said you wanted to see me."

"Thank you for agreeing."

"I didn't think you were asking so much."

"Mrs. Woll did. So did Mrs. Meyer."

"Pardon?"

173

"I called them, too. I wanted to arrange a meeting between the four of us. Three widows of suicides, and me: the two-time loser."

Mrs. Price winced, swallowed, said, "The other young woman . . . Ms. Boone . . . has she . . .?"

"Died? No. She's still in her coma. I spent the morning with her."

"I'm sorry, Mr. Crane. I don't know how you can hold up under it."

"I'm holding up fine. I'm fine."

"You don't look like you slept much last night."

"Neither do you."

"Well," she said, shrugging. "I haven't slept terribly well for over a month. Not since you came around and started me thinking."

"Is that what I did?"

"Of course you did. You know you did. You started me thinking about George. The second George, that is. Well, and the first George, too. They both worked at Kemco. Maybe it killed them both."

"Bet on it."

"You seem very convinced, Mr. Crane."

"Aren't you?"

"I don't know. I know I'm not sleeping. What about the other woman . . . Mrs. Meyer, and who?"

"Mrs. Woll. Neither of them would see me. Either alone, or in a group of the four of us. Mrs. Woll still works at Kemco, and said to get involved would be to risk her job, and after all she has a daughter to raise, and has no suspicions in particular about *her* husband's suicide. Mrs. Meyer didn't give me a reason: she just hung up on me. I take that to mean she's steadfast in her loyalty to her late husband's company."

She shook her head. "How can they ignore it? Suicide upon suicide . . ."

He felt a lump growing in his throat. He sipped the coffee. The lump didn't go away. He put the coffee down. He put a hand to his face. Tears were streaming down his face. He could feel them.

"Mr. Crane . . ."

"I'm sorry . . . I'm sorry . . ."

Then she was beside him, her chair pulled in beside him, and she put an arm around him; comforting him. Patting him.

"I'm sorry, Mrs. Price," he said, better now. "I . . . I guess it just hadn't really hit me yet, about Boone. I'm . . . I'm fine. Maybe it's that I can't believe it, that somebody else is actually acknowledging what's going on."

She scooted her chair away from his a bit, just to give him room, then gave him a warm, weary smile and said, "I don't claim to know what's going on here. But something *is* going on."

"If you and Mrs. Woll and Mrs. Meyer and I were to band together, and contact the Hazardous Waste Strike Force, and any other appropriate or even *goddamnit* inappropriate agencies, and if we'd tell our story to the media, then maybe, just *maybe* something, *something*, would be done."

"Yes, but about what? What really is going on here in Greenwood?"

"Kemco is killing people."

"Be specific, Mr. Crane."

"Boone, and the others, your husband included, stumbled onto something Kemco wanted kept quiet. The illegal hazardous waste dumping, I imagine."

"Are you sure? That's not the sort of crime you go around killing people over."

"Kemco's capable of it. Kemco's capable of anything."

175

"Mr. Crane, you're talking about Kemco as if it were a person, an entity, a monster. That just isn't the reality of it."

"I used to think that way, Mrs. Price. I know the truth now. I'd blow the goddamn place up, if I thought it would do any good. If there weren't a hundred more goddamn plants that would need blowing up as well."

She touched his hand. "Mr. Crane. Try to keep your self-control."

"I am. I'm fine."

"Have you considered that perhaps Ms. Boone's research turned something else up? I know she'd compiled disturbing statistics about diseases among Kemco employees and their families. But I understand there was a fire at her home, not long before she *allegedly* took an overdose of sleeping pills. Was her research material destroyed?"

"Yes."

"If someone is killing people and making it seem like suicide, they're doing a thorough job of it; each victim's been a likely candidate for self-destruction. Is it true her husband had filed for custody of Billy?"

"Yes. Where did you hear that?"

"It's a small town, Mr. Crane."

"So everyone tells me. But nobody seems to be overly concerned about a galloping suicide rate."

"Too many people collect Kemco paychecks, here, Mr. Crane, to get overly concerned about anything. In times like these, a paycheck comes in handy. The suicide rate — and the cancer rate — would have to go considerably higher before Greenwood would wake up."

"I'll wake them up. I'll wake everybody up."

"How?"

He smiled. "You see, I'm the next victim."

"What?"

"I went out to Kemco yesterday. I made myself noticed. So they'll be coming around to see me. To try to make a suicide out of me. Or accident, or whatever. Only I'll be waiting."

"Is that why you didn't sleep last night?"

"I sat up in bed with a gun. And I'll do that every night until they come. And then we'll see. We'll just see."

"Mr. Crane. You've got to get hold of yourself. You should get some rest."

"I'm fine."

"I don't think you really know what's happening here in Greenwood."

"Do you?"

"No. I might have an idea, though."

"Yes? What?"

"I told you you started me thinking. It's about all I've been able to do at night, is think. I drove Harry away—he's the gentleman employed at Kemco, I'd been seeing—and I've jeopardized some longstanding friendships, by asking embarrassing questions of people like Ralph Foster, a local merchant who's the part-time mayor. All because you got me thinking. It made me consider some of the research Ms. Boone has done . . . the illnesses. Take for example the skin rashes. I've seen more children with skin rashes in the last three years than in all my previous years of teaching combined. And then there's the inordinate number of absences we've had at Greenwood Elementary, the past several years. Chronic attendance problems that I think have been misinterpreted. There have been PTA meetings at which parents have been castigated for letting their children play sick. At these meetings always a few indignant parents would insist that they have done no such thing: that a sick child is a sick child and a sick child stays home. But with

177

changing mores in this country, attendance problems have naturally been considered a disciplinary problem, not a health problem."

"I have a friend," Crane said, "who wondered why the children and spouses of Kemco employees would be affected by negligent conditions at a plant twenty-some miles away."

"The same thought occurred to me. Do you remember my mentioning to you that the school is built on ground donated to the city by Kemco?"

"Yes . . ."

"The school grounds, and the playground across the street, as well . . . land given the city twenty years ago by Kemco."

"Yes."

"Do you know what the west edge of Greenwood was, twenty years ago?"

"No."

"A household dump. A landfill. Operated by Kemco, for use by the city as its dump, and for Kemco's own disposal of certain nonhazardous wastes. Or so the mayor told me. But a thought crossed my mind . . . if Kemco is engaging in illegal dumping of hazardous wastes today, a time of environmental concern . . . what do you suppose they were doing twenty years ago?"

Crane was shaking. He felt himself shaking. Was *this* what Mary Beth and the others had discovered? Was this what Boone had discovered? Why her book was burned? Why she now lay in a coma?

"So one has to wonder," Mrs. Price was saying. "What's buried across the street, under the playground? Last month I saw children playing over there — they picked up rocks and threw them at the sidewalk and watched the pretty colors the 'fire rocks' made."

178

He had seen that. Crane had seen that and at the time thought nothing of it: Billy and his friends hurling that rock at the sidewalk and the flash of bright color.

"One has to wonder," Mrs. Price said. She pointed at the floor. "What's buried down there?"

They pulled him out of bed and onto the floor and had the tape over his mouth before he was fully awake.

He didn't remember falling asleep. He'd watched everything there was to watch on television, which had taken him till around two. He'd read some magazines and started a paperback and had read until his burning eyes wouldn't let him read any longer. It wasn't like he hadn't had any sleep: he'd slept for two hours this afternoon, after seeing Mrs. Price. When his travel alarm had woken him, he'd walked downtown to eat at that pizza place again and walked back to the room to watch TV and read and wait in bed with the reading lamp on and the gun in his hand.

The gun was in somebody else's hand, now. It was in the hand of one of the two men who'd pulled him out of bed. The one who had put the tape on his mouth. The other man was beside Crane, on the floor by the bed, tying Crane's hands in front of him.

They wore ski masks, red-and-black, a matched set. The one with Crane's gun was a tall skinny guy in a green-and black-plaid hunting jacket; the other one, standing up now, pulling Crane up by the arm, wasn't as tall, but was wide in the shoulders and wore a black quilted mountain vest and long-sleeved dirty black sweatshirt that hugged his massive arms.

The truckers.

The two men he and Boone had seen dumping drums of waste, in Pennsylvania, weeks ago.

Crane dove head first into the tall skinny guy, gun or no gun, knocking the wind out of him, knocking him down, scrambled over him, got on his feet again, got to the door, but it was closed, and with his hands tied he couldn't open it, and by the time he thought of trying for a window to fling himself through, the bruiser was on him, grabbing both his elbows behind him and pulling his arms back like chicken wings. The pain was sharp; nearly blacked him out.

The skinny one got up, recovered the gun, went over to the lamp. Switched it off. Then he walked to the door, opened it, peeked out, looked to the right, to the left, nodded to the bruiser, who kept hold of Crane's elbows from behind and walked him out into the motel parking lot.

The motel's sign was off. There was no one around; it had to be three-thirty or four in the morning. Still, the two men were cautious. They walked him down to the place where the parking lot went around the back end of the building, where they had parked a battered old pick-up truck, with a couple of steel drums in the back, fifty-five-gallon barrels like the ones the waste had been dumped in.

The skinny one lowered the tailgate and climbed up on the bed of the pick-up. Then the bruiser lifted Crane up to him, like a child from one parent to another, the bruiser's hands on Crane's waist, the skinny guy pulling Crane up and in by one arm, which hurt nearly as much as having his elbows yanked back. He felt an involuntary cry come out of him and get caught by the slash of tape across his mouth.

Then the bruiser climbed up and locked Crane around the waist from behind and lifted him up and

181

set him inside one of the steel drums.

Crane just stood there, the rim coming up to his rib cage, and looked back at the masked faces of the trucker; for the first time he noticed how cold it was: he was in his T-shirt and jeans and it was fucking cold.

Then the bruiser started pushing on Crane's shoulders, shoving him down, and finally Crane got the picture: they wanted him down inside the drum. He resisted for a moment, but it was useless. He crouched within the drum, squeezing himself in, tucking his knees up between the loop of his arms, his hands bound at the wrist by rope, his knuckles scraping the steel of the drum. The steel of its rounded sides seemed to touch him everywhere, in fact, but still he managed to sit, the top of his head six inches or more from the top of the barrel, and he looked up.

And saw the lid coming down.

He couldn't have felt more helpless. The sound of the lid being hammered down wasn't really loud: they were tapping the lid in place with a pair of hammers, doing it easily, not wanting to attract attention; but he never heard anything louder. He never heard anything that echoed so.

He stared up at total blackness.

He sat in total silence.

No, not *total* silence: there was his own breathing, a desperate, snorting sound, breathing through his nose. Already the air seemed stale. Already his muscles seemed cramped. Already claustrophobia was closing in.

Then, another sound: the motor starting up.

Hearing that sound, any sound, was almost reassuring to him.

I'm not dead yet, he thought. *I may be in a steel coffin, but I'm not dead yet.*

He heard the wheels of the pick-up grind against

the gravel of the motel parking lot, then pull onto the street, and the ride began.

Some of it — the first half hour — was on blacktop. The barrel swayed, on the turns, lifting off its bottom tilting just a bit, but never falling over, thanks to the balance he was providing. He began to feel numb. He began not to breathe so hard. The coldness stopped bothering him. He became almost lulled by the darkness, the blacktop road they were rolling over.

Then they hit gravel again, and it was bumpy, and a chuckhole sent the drum clanging into the side of the pick-up and he cracked the side of his head and the pain sent some tears down his cheeks, but the pain wasn't so bad, really. It was something to do.

Is this what death is like? he wondered. *Is it darkness? Is it lack of sensation? Coldness that stops being cold? Pain that stops hurting? Mary Beth, is this death? Boone — is this a coma?*

They were pulling in somewhere, slowing down.

Stopping.

Motor still going.

The door on the rider's side was opening. Someone was getting out. Footsteps on gravel. A gate opening, metallic sounding. Footsteps on gravel again. Back in the pick-up. Door closing.

The pick-up was moving again. Slowly, now.

Then it stopped.

Both doors opened. Footsteps on hard earth. The tailgate was lowered. He heard one of the men hop up onto the bed of the pick-up.

And tipped the barrel over. The side of his head slammed into the side of the drum, stunning him, and then they were rolling him, the barrel and him, and the metal of the pick-up bed and the metal of the drum clashed, and he held his neck muscles tight to keep his head from getting banged.

183

They rolled him only to the edge of the pick-up, then set him down on the ground, rather gently actually.

Then they were rolling him again, and he pulled his neck muscles in tight, but Christ, they were rolling him, rolling him, and he was getting dizzy, so dizzy. . .

Then he felt himself, and the drum around him, go off the edge of something.

It wasn't a long drop. Maybe six feet. The side of him slammed into the side of the barrel, when it landed, but it didn't hurt him. He didn't feel it much. The drum seemed to be sitting at an angle, but he couldn't be sure.

Then he heard one of the men talking to the other. It was the first time he'd heard them speak, but he couldn't make out any of what was being said.

One of the men came down in the hole and straightened the barrel, so that it and Crane were sitting upright. Nice of him.

A few minutes passed. Silence. A certain calm settled over him, as he sat in his drum, in his fetal position, waiting. Waiting for them to kill him.

Then he heard it: something dropping on the top of the lid of the barrel, like rain. Then it was heavier, more like hail.

Dirt.

They were burying him.

He tried to scream, but the tape across his mouth wouldn't let him.

He didn't know how long he'd been buried. The truckers would be gone, by now. He was cold. The stale air seemed to cling to him; so did the darkness. He wondered how long he could last. How long before he would suffocate.

His hands were almost free. He was gradually working one hand down through the knotted loop around his now rope-burned wrists, scraping his knuckles till they bled, which felt good to him, made him feel a little less dead, and then his hands were free and he tore the tape from his lips and began to yell.

Someone would hear him. Someone had to hear.

He yelled until his throat was raw, his voice a hoarse whisper, his ears ringing with the sound he'd made that only he'd heard.

No one would hear him. Who was he kidding? The truckers had obviously dumped him in the country someplace. A landfill, maybe, judging from the sound of the gate that had been opened before the truck drove in to where he'd been dumped. And who would be around at a landfill before dawn, to hear him scream? Nobody. Whoever worked here might come around seven-thirty or eight, but that was hours away; would his air supply last that long? He didn't suppose this thing was airtight, but then he'd heard them filling the hole around him with dirt, and he knew there was dirt over him: no, he'd suffocate before anybody found him. If they found him. Who was to say he'd ever be found at all? Just something else Kemco had buried and forgotten.

He pushed at the lid above him. It seemed to give, a little. A very little, but it did give.

They had hammered that lid down, but maybe he could push up on it and pop the seal, and then maybe he could work the lid off and push it to one side or pull it partially down in with him, and get at the dirt above him, and dig his way out. There couldn't be that much dirt over him; he hadn't dropped that far. A foot or two. He could do it. He could do it.

He pushed with both hands, fingers spread, putting his shoulders into it. And getting nowhere. Again. Harder. Longer.

No.

He sat trying to catch his breath, which wasn't easy in this recycled air. He felt hot, despite the cold; his muscles started to hurt him again, his back was aching. But that was okay: it was better than numbness, and the numbness especially in his arms, was getting worked out.

He put his hands above him, flat, and tried to get his leg muscles into it, tried to stand up, in effect; he pushed up with his legs and put the back of his shoulders up against the lid and his hands slid away and he shoved upward with his whole body.

He kept trying till his body couldn't do it anymore.

And when he sat back down, a sob came out of him, which he quickly swallowed. He couldn't allow himself that: he couldn't let the situation control him; he had to control the situation. He would rest, and try again.

He did, and failed.

He started to cry.

Then he began pummelling the lid above him with his fists, denting the metal. His knuckles began bleeding again. But he was in so restricted an area, a position, that his fists couldn't do much damage, either to himself or the lid. The drum he was in ignored his efforts, his tantrum.

He lowered his head. His shoulders slumped. He sobbed. Loud. Then soft. In some small compartment in his mind, the impartial observer in him sat and recorded it all, seeing it as if from outside, as if this were an experiment he were part of, or perhaps himself conducting, thinking: *so this is despair. This is how despair feels. It isn't just a word.*

He tried to think of what Mary Beth's face looked like but he couldn't bring the image into focus; couldn't exactly remember. He couldn't find her voice, either. And Boone. He tried to see Boone in his mind not in a coma but couldn't. He couldn't. He tried to remember what it was like not to be in this drum. He felt cold. He hugged his arms to himself. His chin touched his chest.

He slept.

He woke.

He was in a hospital: he could smell it around him. He was in a hospital bed. The sheets felt cool. He felt a little groggy. He ached a little. He looked at his hands: they were bandaged.

"Good morning," a voice said.

Crane turned his head slowly and looked at the man seated to his right, near his bed: a guy about thirty with thinning brown hair and gray-tinted glasses; he had on a tan sport jacket with a solid blue tie loose at the neck. He'd been reading a newspaper, waiting for Crane to come around, apparently.

"What hospital is this?" Crane asked. His tongue felt thick.

"Princeton General. In Princeton, New Jersey."

"Who are you?"

"Hart. Sidney Hart."

Crane heard a moaning sound and glanced to his left: a plastic curtain separated him from the other patient in the room, who sounded old.

He turned back to his visitor. "You . . . you're with the Task Force."

"That's right. Hazardous Waste Task Force. Here. Let me crank you up." Hart leaned over and hit a switch; the bed hummed and lifted Crane into a sitting position.

Hart didn't sit back down. "You want anything? Something to drink?"

"Uh. Some juice, maybe?"

Hart rang for the nurse.

While they waited, Crane asked, "Why aren't I dead?"

"Because nobody tried to kill you."

"What?"

"The manager of a landfill a few miles out of Princeton found you in a fifty-five-gallon drum, about seventhirty this morning. The drum was partially buried in a landfill ditch."

"Partially?"

"The drum was covered with dirt on top, and filled in around the sides, but a good fourth of it was exposed to the air. And there were some nail holes in the side, to make sure you got some of that air. Right out in the open, at a busy dumping area."

The nurse came; Hart asked her to bring Crane some juice.

"I don't understand," Crane said.

Hart sat. "You better tell me about it."

Crane did, starting with getting pulled out of bed by the truckers; he didn't mention baiting Kemco.

"Somebody was trying to scare you," Hart said.

"They tried to kill me."

"No. I don't envy you what you went through; but killing you wasn't what it was about."

"Oh?"

Hart shrugged. "They took precautions not to be identified, wore ski masks, never spoke. That indicates they expected you to live through it. So does providing you with air, and leaving the barrel where it couldn't be missed."

"You're not a regular cop. I want to see the regular cops. What are you doing here, anyway?"

"You asked for me."

"I . . . did?"

"In a manner of speaking. You were kind of delirious when they brought you in on the ambulance. But you gave them your name, and said 'hazardous waste' a couple of times, and that was enough to make them call us, in addition to the cops. I was the one who took the call, and I recognized your name. You're the one involved with Anne Boone."

"Yes. And you're the Task Force investigator she talked to."

"Yes. And I kept track of her."

"Then you know where she is now."

"In a coma, in a hospital. At Fair View."

"They tried to kill her, too."

"There's no proof of that, Crane."

"Proof! Jesus! Can't you see what's going on? Can't you fucking see it?"

"I know what you think is going on. I know you think Kemco's involved in some kind of cover-up, and that they're having people killed."

"And making it look like suicide."

"Maybe you can explain what they had in mind when they faked *your* suicide, then. Were we supposed to believe you buried yourself in a barrel?"

"No! No. I . . . don't understand it."

"If Kemco really was having people killed, they'd have had you killed, too. Not gone to elborate lengths to scare you off—*if* Kemco was behind that stunt."

"Scare me! Scare me." He began to laugh. Then he covered his face with a bandaged hand.

Hart stood and put a hand on Crane's shoulder and Crane batted it away.

The nurse came in and gave Crane orange juice and a careful look, Hart a reproving one, left.

"Crane. If there's a cover-up, what exactly's being covered up? Some midnight hauling? Nobody's going to get killed over that. If Kemco got caught at that, they could weather it."

"You don't know, do you? You really don't know."

"What?"

"The landfills in Greenwood! The school, the playground, they're built on landfills that Kemco gave the city, twenty years ago. Supposed to have nothing but harmless shit in it, but you know Kemco."

Hart pursed his lips. Then said, simply: "So?"

"You talked to Boone. You know the statistics: miscarriages, birth defects, illnesses. Maybe the groundwater's been contaminated. Maybe some foul shit is leaching out of twenty-year-old corroded drums and is in the fucking drinking water."

Hart shrugged again. "Possible. Landfills like that are potential hazards, all right, but certainly wouldn't be anything Kemco would bother trying to cover up. Because you can't cover up something like that. What you do is ignore it."

"*You* can't ignore it. It's your job to look for, what did you call it? Potential hazards?"

"Crane, you got it all wrong. My job—the job of the Task Force—is to try to bust Kemco and other offenders in the act of illegal dumping. We got truckers who loosen their tank-truck valves and spill contaminants onto the roadsides. We got midnight haulers who *steal* a truck, load it up with drums, and leave it on a roadside or street. Our job is busting these guys and cleaning up after them. We've got *today* to worry about, Crane. We can't worry about yesterday. That's not what we're paid to do."

"Well, who is, then? The EPA?"

"No. In fact, their unofficial policy is not to seek out hazardous situations."

"What? Why the hell not?"

"Nobody wants to foot the bill, Crane. We've had

191

sixty years of waste dumping in this country and that's about how many billion it would take to clean it all up. Sell *that* to the public."

"That's bullshit! The longer the wait, the more it'll cost to clean that shit up!"

Hart shrugged again. "It's just not going to happen. Nobody in government can afford to go looking for another Love Canal. It's too expensive. And there's plenty of them out there, if you go looking. Officially, there's around 800 'imminent hazard' dump sites. Unofficially it's more like thirty times that many."

"Jesus. Jesus."

"Why don't you go home, Crane?"

"No. This . . . this is just starting."

"It's not starting or stopping. I know what I'm talking about, Crane. This is an ongoing thing. It doesn't end."

"Everything ends."

"Go back to Iowa. You can take your cause with you, if you want. Go to Charles City, Iowa. That wouldn't be a bad place to start."

"Charles City?"

"Familiar with it?"

"I have an aunt living there."

"Charles City. That's where a small pharmaceuticals manufacturer dumped its wastes for years, into a landfill that for some time's been leaching out arsenic, benzene and forty or fifty other poisons into the Cedar River. Know it?"

"My parents have a cottage on the Cedar River."

"That's nice. They'll have a good view of the water source for eastern Iowa getting contaminated. Nothing much is being done to stop it: that small pharmaceuticals company doesn't have the fifty million or so it'll take to fix. You want to help fight this fight? Go home. Fight it there. I'll work on New Jersey, thanks."

192

"They killed Mary Beth. They all but killed Boone. They tried to kill me."

"They. Who the hell is 'they'? Kemco? You're wrong, Crane. Kemco's negligent, and has been for years, and if we can't make 'em clean up their act, we'll shut 'em down, eventually, but they aren't going around faking suicides. It's silly."

Crane made fists out of his bandaged hands. "They tried to kill me!"

Hart sighed, patiently. "Who?"

"Kemco, goddamnit!"

"Specifically, who?"

"Two truckers. The ones Boone and I saw."

"Could you describe them to the police?"

"They . . . had masks."

"Would you recognize them again?"

"Maybe. I don't know. No."

"Did you ever consider the truckers may have done this on their own initiative?"

"What? Why?"

"You and Boone took photographs of them, didn't you? In the act of dumping waste illegally?"

"Yes . . ."

"Well? There's your answer."

"Don't be an asshole! This is all related; can't you see? The suicides. The midnight dumping. Burning Boone's manuscript. What happened to me last night. The landfills the school and playground are on. Hart, you have got to get those landfills checked! They're poisoning that town! Take some soil samples. Do something!"

Hart stood. "I promised Lt. Dean of the Princeton P.D. I'd call him, when you came around. You can give him your statement. It's best it be on the official record. Then, if the doctors'll let you go, I'll put you on a bus back to Greenwood."

193

"Why won't you listen? Why won't anyone listen?"
Hart shook his head and left the room.

In the bed behind the plastic curtain, an old person was moaning.

Crane closed his eyes.

When he got back to his motel room, in Greenwood, the gun was on the bed.

He shut the door. Slipped out of the oversize green jacket they'd given him at the hospital, from their un-claimed lost and found, and walked over to the bed and sat down.

The gun lay in the middle of the bed.

He touched the barrel.

The last time he'd seen it, it had been in the hand of one of the truckers, the skinny one.

What did this mean? A warning? Had the truckers or somebody else from Kemco made a special trip to his room to leave the gun there as a reminder that they could, anytime they liked, reach out and bury him? Or had the truckers, after putting him in the drum in back of their pick-up, tossed the gun back in his room before they left last night?

If they were trying to scare him, it was pointless. After last night, he was past fear. He was past just about everything, except his feelings for Boone, and his feelings about Kemco.

He picked up the gun.

He checked to see if it was still loaded and it was.

He put the gun in his belt, grabbed the hospital's jacket and left.

195

The night was overcast and chilly. There was still snow on the ground. It was only nine o'clock, but there were few cars on the street.

He knocked on Boone's door.

Patrick answered.

"Crane?" He squinted behind the wire frames, as if not recognizing him.

Crane grabbed Patrick by the front of the shirt with both hands and dragged him off the porch and around to the side of the house and tossed him on the snowy ground against some bushes.

"Jesus Christ! Are you crazy? Crane, what's . . ."

Crane got the gun out of his belt and pointed it at Patrick. Patrick's mouth was open.

"They buried me." Crane said.

"Crane . . . what . . ."

"I was dead. Do you want to be dead?"

"I don't know what . . . I . . . Crane . . ."

"They buried me. They burned Boone's book, shoved pills in her. They murdered Mary Beth."

"Crane, you . . ."

"And you're part of it."

"I'm not . . . Crane . . . please . . ."

"You'll be dead when they bury you. That's something."

"Don't do this, Crane!"

"Why not?"

"*Daddy!*"

Billy's voice. From the porch.

Patrick looked at Crane.

Crane looked away.

"Daddy, where are you?"

"Stay where you are, Billy!" Patrick yelled. "Daddy will be there in a second." He looked at Crane. "Won't I, Crane?" Softly.

Crane lowered the gun.

Patrick got up. Dusted the snow off him. "I'm going inside to be with my son, now, Crane."

Crane said nothing.

Patrick went.

Crane walked back to the motel room and sat on the bed. He sat there for two hours.

Then he got up and went into the bathroom and saw himself in the mirror: he was wearing a loose-fitting green jacket, a dirty T-shirt, dirty jeans; he was unshaven; his hands were bandaged; he had several bandages on his forehead. He took his clothes off and the bandages too and had a long hot bath.

Then he got out and sat naked on the edge of the bed and dialed the hospital in Fair View to see how Boone was. Today was the first day since he'd gotten back that he hadn't been to see her. It took a while, but finally he got the doctor and the doctor said her condition was unchanged.

He dialed Roger Beatty, in Iowa City, but there was no answer.

He called his parents. It was an hour earlier back there. His father answered.

"Hello, Dad."

"Son? It's good to hear your voice. We've been so worried about you. Your mother is so worried . . ."

"Is she home?"

"No, bridge club. She should be home any time. She'll be so upset she missed you. Son, please. You have to explain what this is all about. We've got your letter, here, saying you'll be in touch with us, to explain, but . . ."

"Dad. Don't worry about it."

"I . . . don't want to sound like a father, but we're not very happy you dropped out of school. It's your

197

money, of course, and your life, but . . ."

"Dad. I can't talk about that now. Don't worry about that."

"Well. We're not very happy about it, son. Your mother's not very happy."

"I know. I'm sorry. I didn't really call to talk about that, Dad. I just called to let you and Mom know I miss you both."

"Well, we miss you, son. Can you give us an address? A phone number?"

"Tell Mom I love her, Dad. And I love you, too."

He hung up.

He sat naked on the edge of the bed.

He was sitting there with the gun in his hand, finger on the trigger, looking down into the barrel, when somebody knocked on the door.

Patrick.

Standing in the doorway of the motel room in a light tan corduroy jacket that wasn't warm enough for this weather, hands in jacket pockets, shivering, his wire frames fogging up.

"Can I come in, Crane?"

Crane was standing there in jeans he'd pulled on, his chest bare, the gun in one hand.

Patrick noticed the gun. "That . . . that isn't necessary, is it, Crane?"

He wasn't exactly pointing it at Patrick, but to make him feel better, Crane tossed it over on the bed, where it made a thud, and said, "Come in."

Patrick shut the door behind him, took off the wire frames and tried to polish the fog away with his shirt front.

"What do you want, Patrick?"

"Are you all right?"

"I'm fine."

"You seem kind of . . ."

"I'm fine, Patrick. What do you want?"

"I don't know, exactly. Can I sit down or something?"

Crane shrugged. He sat on the edge of the bed and waited for Patrick to do something. Patrick glanced around, saw the chair by the dresser and pulled it over and sat across from Crane. He leaned forward, hands clasped together, draped down between his legs; he looked nervous. Disturbed.

"What do you want, Patrick?"

"I may know something."

Crane didn't say anything.

"I may know who set the fire at the house," Patrick said. It was like a child admitting he'd been in his mother's purse.

Crane's hands tightened into fists; he didn't ask them to, they just did. "Who?"

"I don't know their names or anything . . ."

"*Who*, Patrick?"

"A couple of truck drivers. Some of the neighbors told the police they saw two men, that morning, walking around with ski masks on. Dressed like hunters, is how my one neighbor described them."

"How else did she describe them?"

"One was a tall skinny man. The other was shorter but huskier."

Crane nodded.

"You *know* them?" Patrick asked.

"Sort of. They're the ones that buried me."

"Crane . . . what are you talking about? You said that before, what do you mean, *buried* you?"

Crane told him the story; it didn't take long.

Patrick rubbed his forehead, held the wire frames away from his face as if he didn't really want to see things clearly.

"I . . . don't think they were trying to kill you," he said. "They were just . . . trying to scare you off, I'm . . . sure."

"Wouldn't a beating have sufficed?"

"I think they must've thought that if they . . . stopped just short of killing you . . . really put you through the wringer . . . you'd give up. You'd go home. A simple beating might just spur you on. Convince you you're on the right track."

"What track is that, Patrick?"

"I don't know! I'm speculating. Crane, I'm not really involved in this."

"That's an interesting way to look at it."

"I don't even know if I'm right. But . . . from what you say about what happened to you . . . the burial and all . . . I'm afraid I am. Right, I mean."

"What are you getting at, Patrick?"

He let out the heaviest sigh Crane ever heard. Said, "I think these are the same guys who did some hauling for Kemco, awhile back. I paid them. Cash. All very *sub-rosa*, you know? But that's the extent of my involvement. I had nothing to do with what they did to you. Do you think I'd have my own house burned? Risk my son's life? Or Annie's?"

"Neither one was home, at the time, conveniently enough. And it *wasn't* your house, not till Boone tried to . . ."

"Tried to *what*, Crane? Don't tell me you've come to believe she *did* try to commit suicide? What's changed your mind all of a sudden?"

Crane said, "Who are they, Patrick?"

"I don't even know their names," Patrick said, lifting his shoulders, a pathetic, almost helpless expression on his face. He really *was* trying. "All I know is they work for an outfit called Chemical Disposal Works."

Crane sat up. "In Elizabeth?"

That surprised Patrick. "That's right," he said. "They got in some trouble with the state awhile back, and that's why we had to go under the table with paying them while they were still doing work for us."

"Are they hauling for Kemco, now?"

"Yeah. Right now, in fact. They picked up a load

201

tonight. It might even be those same two truckers, for all I know. It's not a big company."

Crane got up and went to the door and opened it; the cold air rushed in like a wave.

"Thank you, Patrick," Crane said.

Patrick got up slowly, went to the door and said to Crane, "Yeah, well, I should be getting back to Billy. I don't like leaving him alone."

He went out, and as Crane was closing the door, Patrick glanced back and said, "What are you going to do?"

"Change my plans," Crane said.

He had nearly two hours to himself, in the car, on the drive to Elizabeth. It was about midnight when he started out, and there wasn't much traffic on the turnpike; he was in Laurie's car, the Buick she'd been driving him around in, taking him daily to see Boone at the hospital.

When she saw him at the door, Laurie had been momentarily excited, thinking there was some news about Boone; not happy, not frightened, just excited: any news about someone who's been in a coma for a period of time is big news. But that wasn't why he had come; he was there because he needed her car. She started to ask why, but apparently something in his manner had stopped her. She'd merely said, "Of course you can borrow the car," and went and got the keys.

He'd made sure she didn't see the gun; he had it stuffed in his belt, under his jacket, the same jacket the hospital gave him earlier that day, an oversize thing that hung on him like he'd been sick and lost weight.

Now the gun was on the seat next to him.

He wasn't exactly sure what he was going to do with it. Maybe protect himself. Maybe something else. He didn't have it thought out. He didn't think about what he was going to do when he got there. He just drove.

He was aware of something on his face that might have seemed like a smile, to an observer. He wasn't sure what it was himself, when he glimpsed it in the rear view mirror; but it wasn't a smile.

And he wasn't sure what he would do when he faced those two truckers. He just knew he was going to face them.

He wasn't thinking about killing them. The thought surfaced a few times that this was what he might do, but that was as far as his thought processes went. The idea of killing someone would've seemed absurd, impossible to Crane a month ago. A day ago. But now he was different. He had sat on the edge of the abyss and looked in.

By the time he was driving down that industrial stretch, with buildings and machinery and hovering UFO-like gas tanks on either side of him, the night giving all of it an unreal look, like an amusement park, he could hear someone laughing in the car, softly. He was a little surprised to find out it was him.

There were a couple of outdoor lights on poles near the warehouse, but otherwise Chemical Disposal Works was dark. The light from the industrial row Chemical Disposal Works was at the dead-end of, on a little peninsula reaching into an inlet of the Elizabeth River, was enough to let him see the vast city of barrels, stacked four high, at the center of which, like City Hall, was the warehouse with its windows painted out black.

He left the Buick alongside the road, half a block away, gun stuck in his waistband, and soon was walking down the cinder drive he and Boone had come down not long ago, barrels on either side, many of them corroded, leaking; he stepped in a thick puddle of something not unlike molasses in consistency, oozing from the base of one. Up ahead he could see that

204

same tan station wagon parked to the right of the loading-dock area; next to it was a battered, dusty pick-up truck. The pick-up was the one Crane rode in the back of, in a barrel, the night before.

The other truck, the flatbed, wasn't here, unless it was pulled inside.

He didn't think so. It was early yet. Like Crane, the truckers wouldn't have started out till about midnight, and, unless they were going to add to the thirty or so thousand barrels piled in Chemical Disposal's yard, would have to dump their cargo elsewhere. Pennsylvania, maybe. But eventually, he hoped, that truck and the truckers would come home. Home to this graveyard of chemical waste.

He climbed up on the wall of barrels that ended where the side of the building, and the loading-dock area, started. He sat on a barrel with the gun in his hand, resting in his lap, and waited. It was cold, and the hospital hand-me-down jacket, loose fitting as it was, did little to keep the cold out; but Crane didn't mind. He liked it.

He counted stars: there weren't many to count. A piece of the moon floated half-heartedly in a sky streaked by smoke from nearby industrial chimneys. He could smell more of the river, tonight, than during his daytime visit; but the sickly perfume laced with rubber was still thick. Boone had explained to him that this was an odor characteristic of dump sites.

He thought about her. He thought about her as long as he could do it without seeing her in a coma; when that image came into his mind, he forced it out.

He counted barrels.

He'd been sitting there perhaps an hour when headlights stretched down the cinder drive, a truck rumbling after.

It was the same flatbed truck, its sides built up, its

205

tarp flapping, that he and Boone had seen at Kemco that time. Even from here he could see two men in the cab.

He hopped off the barrels, landed hard, and caught himself with the hand that didn't have the gun in it.

Then he walked out in the path of the truck, stopped in front of it, and it stopped, too, abruptly, brakes squealing, a good two car lengths between them, but he could see their faces behind the windshield, clearly. They were faces he'd never seen close-up before, not without ski masks in the way, but that the driver was the tall skinny man and the rider the stocky one was apparent. So was the look of fear on their faces, as he pointed the gun at them.

The stocky one looked a bit like his friend Roger, which threw him a little, and the skinny one had a long, roughly handsome face and dark curly hair and was young, about Crane's age, and that threw him, too: he was so used to a faceless enemy, it shocked him to be confronted by two people, that it should all boil down to two young men as scared at this moment as he was.

Because his finger was squeezing the trigger, but he couldn't make it squeeze hard enough — in his mind, he could hear their cries of pain and surprise, but he couldn't seem to make his finger turn those mental images and sounds into reality.

Something cold crawled into his stomach; something colder crawled into his mind: he couldn't kill these people. He'd forced this confrontation and he didn't know what to do with it.

"Get out!" he yelled. "Get out of that goddamn truck!"

The doors on either side swung open, but neither man hopped out.

Crane heard a door open behind him, at his left,

and he turned halfway and saw the man in the quilted jacket with the bushy black streaks for eyebrows who had given him that beating not so long ago. The man did not seem to be armed, though he probably wished he was. He was standing frozen in the doorway by the loading dock, looking at the gun, which Crane was now pointing his way.

"Take it easy, kid," the man was saying.

Whether or not he recognized Crane, Crane couldn't tell; he did recognize the gun, however, and kept on saying "Take it easy, take it the fuck easy, okay?" like a litany.

Crane heard the truck's doors slam shut. The distraction had been just enough to give the truckers what they saw as an opportunity: the vehicle was moving, the driver aimed its prow right at Crane, the vehicle shifting noisily as it bore down on him.

There was just enough space between them and Crane for the truck to work some speed up, and it was just confined enough an area for Crane to wonder where the hell to go; the walls of barrels were everywhere, except in the loading dock, which was just another wall to get rammed against, and the cinder drive, where the truck was.

He didn't shoot at them. He was too busy running, and then there was nowhere to go and his back was to the wall of barrels and they were coming right at him, and he dove and rolled, rolled out of the way, and the truck smashed into the wall of barrels and the explosion was immediate.

A bright orange fist of fire shot into the sky, and hung there, and shook as if in anger. Crane was blown by the force of it against the far wall of barrels, away from the flames. Behind him, the screams of the truckers were cut short with the second spasm of fire and smoke.

Crane was up and running, gun still in hand, the heat and flames to his back, but he could hear the sound of it, like heavy artillery shells going off, and when he did look back, there were barrels hurtling themselves into the air, hundreds of feet, some tumbling end over end, trailing smoke and fire, others bursting like bombs in a fireworks display of horrifying proportions.

The shape of the truck, at the base of the burning wall of barrels, was only barely discernible, the warehouse a black silhouette with windows of red-orange, its roof on fire; where the guy with the black streak eyebrows had gone, Crane didn't know — if he ducked back inside when the truck went after Crane, he was gone, period. Flames had spread to the pick-up and were on their way past the loading dock to the adjacent wall of barrels, and Crane ran, barrels dropping behind him like bodies out of high windows; he could hear them, thudding to the ground, when the sound of barrels exploding wasn't obscuring all else.

The Buick was up ahead, and he wondered if he could make it; if the fire spread to those silver, hovering gas tanks, so very close to the blaze, there could be a firestorm, and a city — a real one, not populated by waste drums — might die.

Then something behind him exploded loudly and the blast drove him face down, onto the cinders, scraping his face, and he suddenly realized his jacket was on fire, and he got out of it somehow, ran out of it, and it fell to the ground behind him, waving its fiery arms. He stood there looking up into a sky full of fire, from which barrels fell as if dropped from a plane, and his legs went out from under him, and darkness came.

five
aftermath

30

The first major snowstorm of the winter had been just three days ago, but the roads were clear and so was the afternoon. Even with his tinted glasses, the sun reflecting off the pavement bothered his eyes. But otherwise Hart felt pretty good. Today was kind of special: he'd had some good news for a change.

He was stretching a point, driving down here on company time. The Greenwood situation was out of his hands, now, which was fine with him. He'd gotten some glory out of it, which is to say some nice press notices, and now Greenwood was the combined headache of the state of New Jersey and the U.S. Government, specifically the NJ Health Department and the EPA.

Of course, that crazy kid Crane had been wrong about a lot of things. There was no Kemco conspiracy as such, no cover-up in which employees who "knew too much" were murdered as phonied-up suicides. Like he'd told the kid, that was absurd.

But Crane had been dead right about those landfills. Hart had been haunted by the hysterical kid's ranting about those damn things, and, even though it wasn't really his bailiwick, he'd gone ahead and had the soil samples taken and chemical tests made. He'd expected the findings to be routine. They weren't.

For what had supposedly been used for a household

dump, the landfills below Greenwood Elementary School and its playground were a toxic nightmare: seventy dangerous chemical substances, a dozen of them known carcinogens. Including Benzene, harbinger of leukemia. Including dioxin, which made Benzene look like health food.

As for the city's drinking water, it had been tested previously, of course — for bacteria. When tested for chemicals, Greenwood's tap water turned out to be a cocktail containing high levels of synthetic compounds that were known carcinogens and extremely toxic. The only reason tests for bacteria came up clean was that there was so much pesticide in Greenwood's water, no bacteria could survive.

The wells supplying the city's water were sealed off; while a new source was sought, Greenwood citizens were told not to use the water for drinking or cooking. The bottled water business boomed.

The Governor came to Greenwood, after declaring it a state disaster area.

The President of the United States came, too, and watched for fifteen minutes as the remedial drainage program was getting under way. He had not declared Greenwood a national emergency, as another President had at Love Canal, and Hart knew why: EPA officials had advised this President that he simply couldn't go around declaring an emergency every time one of these environmental time bombs went off, not unless he was ready to make a habit of it.

And the President of Kemco had said only that "we do not believe we have any legal liability."

Dream on, sucker, Hart smiled to himself.

The current investigation, sparked by that crazy Crane's efforts, had linked Kemco to Chemical Disposal Works, and it was the disaster at Chemical Disposal that had served to bring the state's — hell, the nation's—attention to the waste problem. The death toll had been three; the injured (including workers at close by industrial sites, and fire fighters) totalled nearly forty—with far worse statistics narrowly averted when the entire 250-man fire department of Elizabeth, New Jersey, fought the flames for ten tiring hours, keeping the fire from reaching tanks of liquid gas nearby.

The toxic smoke from the fire had drifted to New York City, which attracted attention to say the least, and New Jersey was forced, at last, to clean up Chemical Disposal. Men wearing special suits with oxygen masks, looking like something out of *2001*, were even now cleaning up the site, in 12-hour, 7-day-a-week shifts.

Well, at least the pile of drums at Chemical Disposal had finally dwindled, though this was a hell of a way to get that done. It had cost the state, so far, $5 million, not to mention the endangering of thousands of lives. Due to the dangerous nitric and picric acids, pesticides and plasticizers that were among the *known* surprises in the barrels, schools were closed in Elizabeth and Staten Island, and residents were urged to stay home with windows closed, till the toxic clouds blew away. And now on to the 233 other problem sites identified in New Jersey—only 23 of which were funded as "target sites."

The hospital was just inside Fair View's city limits. Hart pulled into the lot, parked, went in and asked at the information window where Intensive Care was.

He got in the elevator and pressed "4," and when the doors opened, he saw Mrs. Alma Price, the attractive, redhaired middle-aged schoolteacher who'd been so helpful to him when he was doing the preliminary investigation of the landfill situation. She was sitting reading a magazine (*Psychology Today*) on one of the couches grouped opposite the elevators.

"Mrs. Price," he said, sitting next to her. "How are you?"

"Very well," she smiled, putting the magazine down. "I take it you're here because you heard the good news?"

"Certainly am. And I take it you're waiting to get in, yourself?"

She nodded. "Only one visitor at a time. Haven't seen you around Greenwood in a few weeks."

"That mess is out of my hands, now, thank God. Where are you holding classes, these days?"

"We've set up shop in several church basements. Tell me . . . why haven't any homes been evacuated? A number border the playground landfill. With the drainage started, won't fumes be a problem? Weren't two or three hundred families relocated, when this occurred at Love Canal?"

"Mrs. Price, this isn't precisely the same thing as Love Canal. We caught it earlier, thanks to your friend Crane. That's one difference. But I'd say there's still a chance some of the homes'll have to be evacuated."

She shook her head. "When I think of the suffering . . . I don't know. I could weep. I *have* wept."

"That suffering you're talking about has already been confirmed by a Health Department official," Hart said. "His report confirmed Ms. Boone's research for her book — ailments ranging from as minor as skin rashes to as major as respiratory disease."

"What about the psychological aspects?"

Hart shrugged. "I don't think that's been dealt with yet. But it's going to have to be. I'm no scientist, but the presence of dioxin makes anything possible. Dioxin is known to create psychological disturbances . . . which might help explain twelve nervous breakdowns in Greenwood in eighteen months."

"It would also help explain one other thing," Mrs. Price said.

214

"Yes?"

"The suicides."

Hart nodded. "I believe you may be right. Crane and Boone never thought to connect the disproportionate suicide rate to the similarly high rates of miscarriage and so on. They assumed the suicides were fakes. But there was that one instance of suicide — the guy who killed his wife and kids, and then himself, in front of a witness — that clearly *wasn't* faked."

"And neither were the other ones. My husband included."

He touched her hand. "Your husband, and the others, were people with legitimate reasons to be depressed. But who normally might've been able to deal with their depression."

"And you think it was the effect of the chemically contaminated water, here in Greenwood, that . . . pushed them over the edge?"

"That's my opinion, yes. Take for example a guy who's had a nervous breakdown or two, got a Section Eight out of the service. He's a trucker for Kemco, now, and knows what kind of dumping's been going on. Maybe he's done a little of it himself. Then one day he learns his wife has a tumor in her head the size of a shotgun shell. And that night he kills her, and his kids, and himself."

"Lord."

"Look at Crane himself, the direction his behavior took; he'd been here long enough to be affected himself, to exhibit decidedly suicidal behavior. But Boone and Crane had it in their heads that Kemco was going around killing people."

"Weren't they? Aren't they?"

"Well, yes. They're guilty of criminal negligence, no question. But they're big. It's hard to hurt a corporation that size; you'd be surprised the sort of lawsuits they can absorb with minimum pain. It helps that both the Chemical Disposal fiasco and the scandal of the schoolyard landfills broke at the same time. Doesn't paint a very pretty picture of Kemco yesterday or today. Still, Kemco will survive."

"I don't understand you, Mr. Hart. You have so little bitterness when you speak of Kemco. Perhaps Kemco wasn't having people murdered, in the sense of hiring it done, like the Mafia or some such thing. But in a way, what they've done is worse . . . it's invisible . . . intangible . . . and those responsible are so removed from it all. So protected."

Hart shrugged again. "They're just businessmen trying to make a dollar, and I got nothing against that. I don't approve of how they're going about it, but did you ever consider this? The Kemcos of this world are only here because we want them. Okay, we found some landfills that were contaminating Greenwood's water supply, putting sickness, physical and mental, into every glass of water every citizen and visitor to the city drank for God knows how long. We found those landfills and are doing something about it. But there are thousands, tens of thousands more Greenwoods and Love Canals out there. And maybe we can find them, and do something about them. But they're all yesterday's waste. What about today's? I remember telling Crane that I couldn't be too concerned about yesterday because I was watching out for today, and do you know what we're doing today, this year? Dumping 77 million pounds of waste into the environment. Know what we'll be doing next year? Dumping 77 million more. There's suicide for you. Maybe instead of putting all the blame on the Kemcos, foul as some of them are, we should look for ways to improve or curb or even stop the type of manufacturing that creates such waste. Maybe a whole new life-style

216

is called for, who knows? I don't. I like my car. I like all the great American luxuries. But you know what else I like? I like a glass of water that doesn't give me cancer, or send me into the bathroom to slash my wrists if I have an off day.'

Mrs. Price sat and looked at him with a quiet smile. She said, "Would you be embarrassed if I said I misjudged you?"

Embarrassed, Hart stood. "Where's that room, anyway? I'm going to peek in. Rules be damned."

Mrs. Price pointed down the hall to the right. "Room 417."

"Thanks. See you in a few minutes."

He passed several doctors and three or four nurses, but no one stopped him; and at room 417, he opened the door, went in and there was Boone, sitting up in her bed, an I.V. hooked up to her, looking thin, pale, beautiful.

Crane was sitting next to her. Holding her hand. He was in street clothes; he'd been released from the hospital, for treatment of minor but extensive burns, yesterday. They both looked very happy, if battle-scarred.

"Hello, you two," Hart said. "I just wanted to welcome Ms. Boone back among the living."

Boone said, in an amazingly strong voice, "It's nice to be back."

"I need to talk to both of you. I'm going to need to get a deposition from you, Ms. Boone. I already have Crane's — and considering some of the things he pulled, he's lucky no charges are being brought against him."

Crane said, "Don't do me any favors."

"Why not? You've done us a few. Anyway, Ms. Boone, it can wait. What are your immediate plans, now that you're uh . . . with us again?"

217

"Well," she began.

Crane interrupted. "We have a book to write."

"Yes," Boone said. "I guess we do at that."

Hart smiled, said, "Happy royalty checks," and went out.

He walked down the hospital hall, thinking about how much he liked happy endings.

He wondered how this one would come out.

author's note

The events in this novel are not true, but they of course have parallels in reality — from Love Canal to the disaster in April 1980 at Chemical Control Corporation in New Jersey. Nonetheless, this novel should be viewed as an entertainment and not as nonfiction, and those seriously interested in the toxic-waste problem should seek out the numerous magazine and newspaper articles available, as well as Michael Brown's definitive *Laying Waste* (Pantheon, 1980).

I was particularly aided by two television documentaries, the transcripts of which were kindly provided to me by their producers: Nova, "A Plague on Our Children," 1979, WGBH, written, produced and directed by Robert Richter; and ABC News Closeup: "The Killing Ground," 1979 (and a later 1980 update), written by Brit Hume, Michael Connor and Steve Singer, directed by Tom Priestly, produced by Priestly and Singer. Also, various representatives of both federal and local environmental agencies provided much appreciated help.

I would like also to thank my agent, Dominick Abel; and my editor at Foul Play Press, Lou Kannenstine.

Finally, I would like to thank my wife, Barbara Collins, for convincing me to write this one and for staying at my side for what proved a long midnight haul.